I0451069

Worthy of Love

Other Books by Author

Girl, Naw!
It Ain't Over

Journey to Love

Sophomore Mom

The Christmas Gift (short story)

First Lady Series
Positive Deception
Lina's Redemption (coming Spring 2018)

**Available in Print and Digital format
At online retailers and bookstores**

Worthy of Love

LaCricia A'ngelle

www.hispenpublishing.com

Douglasville, Georgia

This book is a work of fiction. The characters, incidents, and dialogues are products of the author's imagination and are not to be construed as real. Any references to actual events, persons, living or dead, or to real locales are intended to give the novel a sense of reality.

Worthy of Love

Published by His Pen Publishing, LLC
Douglasville, Georgia 30135
www.hispenpublishing.com

Copyright ©2018 by LaCricia A`ngelle

Cover design by HPP Designs
The scanning, uploading, and distribution of this book without permission is a theft of the author's intellectual property. If you would like permission to use material from the book (other than for review purposes), please contact publisher@hispenpublishing.com. Thank you for your support of the author's rights.

ISBN: 978-1-944643-01-0

Library of Congress Cataloging-in-Publication Data is available

First Printing January 2018

This book is also available in digital eBook format

Dedication

This book is dedicated to
My mother, sisters, and daughters

To all the single women that are over 40
that believe love is still possible
this book is for you

Acknowledgments

Above all, I give Praise and Honor to my Heavenly Father. Lord you are AMAZING! All That I am, and all that I have is because of you.

To my husband, Christopher. Thank you for believing in me and for constantly giving me your unwavering support. I love and appreciate you.

To my mother and biggest fan, Emma. It's because of you that I have the strength and courage to be the woman God called me to be. To my Pop, Murry. Thank you for always reminding me to just pray. To my daddy, Felix in Heaven. Look at your baby girl! I love you all, and without a doubt I have the greatest parents ever!

To my big sister Felicia. Thank you for always having my back and cheering me on. To my other sisters Angie, Kerri, Diane, and Kim thank you for loving me and being there when I need you.

To my children Keshonna, Larry, Denajae, Ayonna, Gabrielle, Samantha, and my g-baby Landon. I love you and I pray I am a constant inspiration and example to you. Know that you all are Worthy of Love and that I love you all more than words.

To my Bestie Shelia. What can I say. Because of you, my writing has grown tremendously. I thank God for you, not only in my writing career but also in life. You are the true definition of a best friend. I love you She-She.

To my Pastor and First Lady, Wilbur and Kimberly Purvis. Thank you for being an awesome example and ministering to me without ceasing. Thank you for your prayers and for extending to me opportunities beyond my imagination. I thank God for you and the Destiny World Church family.

To our dear friends Clay and Dorothy Horton. I praise God for the day he sent you both into our lives. Your friendship has been a tremendous blessing. We love you.

To all of you wonderful readers. Thank you for taking the time out to read my novels. You are a constant inspiration. You bring joy to me, and for that I am grateful. Know that you are constantly in my thoughts and prayers. I love you all.

"What do you mean, this is your wife!" Iris yelled, pushing Christian's hand away as he attempted to help her get up. Her legs swished across the floor causing her high heel shoes to scar the freshly waxed floor.

"Mom, this is ridiculous. Let me help you up," he urged.

"Don't you touch me," she insisted, rolling over onto her knees and using the couch to boost herself up.

Iris stood and straightened her burgundy sheath dress. She smoothed her hair, gently tucking it on the ends. Placing her hand on her pearls, she took a deep breath. Iris collected herself as much as possible before turning her attention to Shelby.

She carefully examined the woman standing before her. She would never admit how beautiful Shelby was. Instead she chose to focus on Shelby's deception. She spied the mid-thigh length white dress with the sheer overlay littered in pink and yellow flowers.

How country can she get? Iris thought.

Shelby stood stiff, holding Christian's arm tightly. She took shallow breaths in silence, watching the scene before her unfold.

Christian stood beaming. His smile was that of a proud groom.

1

"When did you do this? How did you do this? Why did you do this?" Iris folded her arms and glared at Christian and Shelby. "Are you pregnant?" she asked Shelby with a look of disgust.

"I beg your pardon," Shelby snapped back. She could understand Christian's mother being upset, but she was not going to be disrespected.

"Mom, stop. Shelby is not pregnant." He raised his palms in an effort to calm the ladies down. "I married her because I love her. We got married this morning before we left Tennessee. We eloped so there was no one there but the preacher, his wife, and Shelby's mother."

Christian immediately regretted mentioning Shelby's mother.

"Son, I believe we need to talk, and I mean right now."

"We can talk in front of Shelby. After all, she's my wife now."

"Stop calling her that," Iris yelled. "I told you to find somebody to keep company with while you were there. That meant go to dinner, or the movies, or whatever you all do these days. That did not mean bring the woman back with you. What on earth were you thinking, son. This has to be the cruelest joke you have ever played."

"I'm not joking, Mother. Shelby is my wife, and your new daughter."

"Humph. We'll see about that."

Iris bent down and snatched her purse from the couch, tucking it under her arm. She rolled her eyes at Shelby before pushing through the two of them and causing them to separate. She stumped to the front door. Her heels violently clacked against the floor with each step. Yanking the door open, she stormed out, slamming it behind her.

2

"Whelp, that went well," Christian said to a shocked Shelby.

"Excuse me?"

"Yeah. She took it better than I thought. Don't get me wrong, my mother is very prim and proper but she has been known to start swinging at times when she really gets upset. We got off easy."

Christian smiled and tugged on Shelby's arm. "Now where were we before she got here?"

Shelby pulled back. "Christian, this isn't funny. I don't see how you can make light of this situation. Your mother is clearly upset. She asked me if I was pregnant as if that's the only reason you would marry me. In fact, she almost knocked me down when she pushed between us. This is not how I wanted to start our life together. You're smiling and trying to go back to business as usual like it's no big deal. And don't think I didn't hear her say you were supposed to find someone to spend time with while you were there. I guess I know where I stand."

"Sweetheart, that's ridiculous. I married you, so obviously you weren't just someone to help me pass the time." Christian turned Shelby towards him and placed his hands on her shoulders. "Everything will be fine. My mother will get used to our marriage. Don't worry, she'll warm up to you and grow to love you as much as I do."

He placed a gentle kiss on her lips, hoping to relax her. Shelby tried to resist but eventually she succumbed to Christian's advances. The fact remained she was his wife in every way. After meeting Iris, it seemed obvious the woman would not make things easy for them but Shelby was determined to make their marriage work.

She placed her arms around Christian's neck and pulled

him closer. With a low moan, she kissed him with all the passion a woman in love could produce.

Iris sat in her car fuming. The anger she felt towards her son burned within like a consuming fire. Beads of sweat formed on the tip of her nose. She was convinced Christian had played a cruel joke on her. There was no way he would marry a woman he couldn't have known very long. The whole idea was preposterous.

Peering at the front door to Christian's house, she waited for him to come rushing out. She'd made a dramatic exit knowing he would follow her outside to appease her. Minutes passed and Christian still had not stepped outside, causing Iris' anger to overflow. She looked down at her steering wheel and contemplated laying on the horn to force her son out of the house, but quickly reconsidered. She was appalled but she still had an image to uphold. He had to have known she was still outside. She wanted to march back inside to give him a piece of her mind, but she was too angry to move.

Her mouth dropped when she saw an image of Christian chasing Shelby past the large picture window in the living room heading in the direction of his downstairs master suite. Disgusted, she started her car and drove around the circular driveway, exiting the property. Iris issued a final threat, that only she could hear. "If this is how you want to play it, get ready for the consequences."

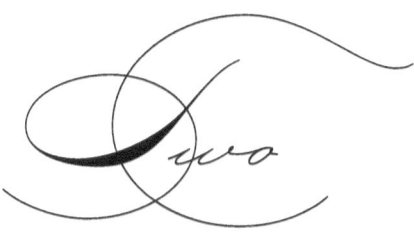

Shelby awoke feeling refreshed. She couldn't recall ever sleeping as peaceful as she had on her first night with Christian. She stretched her body, basking in the silkiness of the sheets. Shelby glanced over her shoulder and admired her husband's physique as she reminisced on their intimate moments. While they were dating, she had imagined what it would be like when she and Christian consummated their marriage. They had shared intimate moments in Tennessee that left her wanting him, but Christian never crossed the line with her. A satisfied grin spread across her lips.

"Definitely worth the wait," she whispered.

Easing out of the bed, Shelby made her way to the bathroom to freshen up. She never was the domestic type but she wanted to prepare Christian a delicious breakfast in bed. She showered and put on a short silk robe. She exited the room in complete silence with the aid of the thick plush carpet. Taking a final glance at Christian, she noticed he hadn't moved at all. She mentally planned her meal as she made her way to the kitchen.

"Shouldn't you put some clothes on? Ugh," Iris rolled her eyes and turned up her nose in disgust at Shelby as she entered the kitchen.

Shelby screamed to the top of her lungs, startled by Iris' unexpected presence. "What are you doing here?"

5

"I could ask you the same thing, but I'm sure I already know the answer to that question."

Shelby pulled her robe closed. "How long have you been here?"

Christian came running down the stairs carrying a baseball bat. He stopped at the entrance of the kitchen and looked back and forth between his wife and his mother. "Mom, what are you doing?"

"I brought you some groceries. I figured you hadn't taken time to go and get any since you got home yesterday. I knew you'd be otherwise occupied," Iris stated, rolling her eyes at Shelby.

Disgusted, Shelby stormed out of the kitchen and headed back to her upstairs Grand Master bedroom.

Christian sat down in a nearby chair, placed the bat on the counter, and gave his mother a hard stare.

Iris removed a carton of eggs from the grocery bag and placed them inside the refrigerator. Next, she reached for a quart of milk and proceeded to put it away.

"Mother," Christian called out in a commanding tone.

"What is it?" Iris snapped back, slamming the milk carton down on the refrigerator shelf.

"Are you seriously going to pretend like you haven't done anything wrong?"

Iris turned around to face Christian. She placed her left hand on her hip and pointed at him with her right hand. "Wrong? I haven't done a thing wrong. As a matter of fact, you need to be thanking me instead of taking that tone with me. How was I to know the little hussy you brought here would be half naked."

"Mom, I know you're not happy about me getting married and not telling you, but you're being ridiculous.

This is my house and even though you may not like Shelby, you do need to respect her as my wife."

"Oh, so that's what this is all about. You're choosing her over me? Someone you have only known a couple of months."

"It's not about choosing. She's my wife and you're my mother. If you would give her a chance I'm sure you will find that you like her. You refuse to give her a shot and I have no idea why."

"Why, Christian?"

"Huh?"

"Why? I just want to know why you would do this. Why would you go off and marry a woman that you don't even know? You knew you were wrong, otherwise you would have told me. My only child got married, and I wasn't invited. Do you know how badly that hurts? Did you consider me at all?"

Christian dropped his head. He was so excited about marrying Shelby that he never stopped to consider how his mother would feel about not being a part of his marriage ceremony. He was more concerned about her disagreeing which is why he chose to keep it secret until after the marriage was official.

"Mom, I'm sorry. I should have informed you so that you could witness me and Shelby getting married."

Iris walked over to Christian and placed her hand on his shoulder. "What's done is done, son. I forgive you. Just please tell me you at least got her to sign a prenup."

Christian eased her hand off his shoulder. He stood and stepped to the other side of the kitchen.

Iris surveyed his actions. "You have got to be kidding me."

Christian remained silent.

She threw her hands up in the air and shook them vigorously. "Have you not learned anything? You know what, that's okay. We can fix this. I'll call our family attorney and have him to draw up a postnup. We'll get this cleared up right away. Don't worry about it son, mama's got you."

"No," Christian stated firmly. "Please, Mother, stay out of this. I know what I'm doing. The only thing I need you to do is to get to know Shelby. And for goodness sake, give me back my key."

"Oh, now you want your key back, too? And you're going to act like you're not changing. Fine."

Iris removed the key to Christian's house from her key ring and tossed it across the counter towards him. Leaving the remaining grocery in the bags, she turned towards him and shook her head in disgust.

"Never in a million years could I have seen this coming. I hope you know what you're doing Christian. Because with the way I see it. This will be a disaster."

"You'll just have to trust me, Mother."

Christian reached for Iris to pull her into an embrace, but she backed away.

"I'm sorry, son. I can't be a part of this. I have to go." She gathered her things and left as quietly as she entered.

Christian inhaled and blew the air out of his lungs forcefully. A part of him wanted to go after his mother, but he knew he couldn't. He had an angry wife to contend with.

"It's too early in the morning for this," he grumbled.

Shelby grabbed her suitcase and paced the length of the room while gathering her clothes. She couldn't imagine how she could be so stupid, leaving her life behind, thinking Christian was her Prince Charming. She was expecting a bed of roses but from the looks of it, she had fallen into a bed of thorns. She and Christian had been married less than forty-eight hours and his mother was already making life difficult.

After tossing the last batch of clothing into her suitcase, she sat on the bed and looked around the room. From the moment Christian gave her the grand tour she had fallen in love with her new home. She thought her dreams had finally come true. Unfortunately, Christian's mother was making it a pure nightmare.

She could only imagine the conversation Christian was having with his mother downstairs. She was tempted to return to the kitchen to listen in, but quickly reconsidered. It would be great if he was defending her and their marriage, but she would be mortified if he wasn't. Feeling overwhelmed, she picked up her cell phone and called the one person she believed could help. The phone barely rang before the call was connected.

"I know you're not calling me now, heifah."

"Hey, Kim, girl. How you doing?"

"Don't be 'hey Kimin' me. Especially after I saw Ms. Linda at the grocery store, and she told me you done got married, and up and moved to California. Really, Shelby? I thought we were supposed to be best friends."

"I'm sorry, Kim. Everything happened so fast. Christian and I eloped."

"Dang, girl. That's messed up."

"I know, I'm sorry. But it may be over before it ever gets started. I need your help. For real."

"What's going on? Don't tell me that man is mistreating you already."

"No, he's not, but I can't take his mama. Let's just say she is not here for this marriage. Girl, she asked if I was pregnant, then this morning she showed up unannounced talking about I need to put some clothes on when I went downstairs to make him breakfast."

"Ooh. You got one of those mother-in-laws. I feel for you. I mean why is she so mad? Didn't he tell her he was getting married?"

Shelby fell silent on the phone.

"Shelby!" Kim exclaimed. "I know y'all didn't get married without telling his mama. Please don't tell me that."

"Ok, I won't tell you."

"No wonder the woman is pissed. Girl, you might as well get ready because you are in for it."

"Kim, this is serious. I got so upset today that I packed my suitcase. I think I've made a huge mistake. I'm thinking about coming home until I start school."

"I am being serious, Shelby. That woman is going to give you the blues. Especially if he's her only son, or youngest son."

"He's her only child," Shelby said solemnly.

"That's worse."

"See, that's exactly why I think it's best if I leave."

Kim paused before replying to Shelby. "Do you love him, Shelby?" she asked sincerely.

"I really do, Kim. I want nothing more than to be married to Christian. I love him so much."

"Then fight, Shelby. We both know you ain't no punk. I mean, try to win her over, but most importantly focus on being a great wife. When a woman sees that you are good to her child she eventually comes around. You've been married what, two days? It's way too early to give up, especially if it's not because of a problem between you and him."

"I wish you could see this place, Kim. It is way more than I could've imagined."

"Girl, me and Julian might have to fly out there and check it out. I have always wanted to visit L.A."

"That would be cool. I can't believe we are both married women now. That seems so funny. Well, married for now."

"What do you mean married for now?" Christian asked, interrupting her telephone conversation.

Shelby snapped her head towards the door. She didn't realize Christian had entered the room. She wondered how much he had heard. Shelby watched as his eyes scanned the room and landed on her suitcase.

"What's going on, Shelby? What's with the suitcase?"

She looked at the phone in her hand and realized Kim was still on the line. "Hey, Kim, I need to call you back, girl."

Kim started laughing. "Okay, girl. Welcome to married life." Kim continued laughing until the call disconnected.

Christian stood looking at Shelby, waiting on an explanation. With a tone more elevated than normal, he asked, "Shelby, are you going to answer me or what?"

11

"Wait a minute, Christian. Don't take that tone with me. I have every right to be upset."

"Okay, so if you're upset we talk about it. You don't pack a suitcase and call people telling them you're leaving."

Shelby rolled her eyes. "What do you expect, Christian? I was insulted in what is supposed to be my home. Your mother told me I needed to put some clothes on. Do you know how embarrassing that was?"

Christian stepped towards Shelby. She jumped up from the bed and moved away from him. She knew he was trying to comfort her, but she was not ready to be comforted. This was her moment to express herself and she refused to allow him to simply hug it away.

"I can't live like this, Christian. I won't live like this. Constantly looking over my shoulder, not feeling free to walk around my own home, wondering if your mom or someone else has free reign. I can't do it."

Christian held out his hand and revealed the key he was holding.

"What is that?" Shelby snapped.

"It's the key to our home. I took it from my mother. She no longer has access to the house, unless we invite her in. I want you to have it." Christian stepped closer to Shelby. "You need to know I'm in this marriage completely. I love you, Shelby, and we will make this work. My mother is upset about not being a part of our wedding. I get that she's mad, but as I told her, you are my wife and I won't let her or anyone else come between us."

"So, is this how it's going to be? Me constantly having to look over my shoulder, wondering when she's going to pop up? She hates me, Christian."

"She doesn't hate you. She doesn't even know you." Once

again, he reached for her. "Let's not do this. We can't start our marriage off like this. We had a great night, and I want it to continue."

He pulled Shelby into his arms and felt her resistance fading. Holding her tightly, he attempted to comfort her. It wasn't a time for words. He was caught between an upset and angry mother, and a wife that shared the same feelings. Christian looked up as Shelby relaxed in his arms and whispered, "Please fix this."

Four

Iris sat at the coffee shop patiently awaiting her friend Melissa's arrival. She was already on her second cup of coffee. She contemplated switching to decaf when she realized her right knee was still jumping. She didn't know if it was from the coffee or her nerves. She always knew Christian going to Tennessee would end up in disaster. She'd tried to warn him but he didn't listen. Sure, the youth center had been built, but the excess baggage he brought back was totally unnecessary.

She looked up to see Melissa coming through the door. Iris raised her hand and beckoned her over to the table. She stood and stepped away from her chair, greeting her friend with a warm embrace.

Once the ladies were seated, Ina, a curly haired waitress approached the table. Her red tresses were pulled into a loose ponytail. With a small tablet in hand, she greeted the ladies with her usual smile. She had gotten to know Iris and Melissa quite well in the two years she had worked at the swanky Beverly Hills coffee shop. She first directed her attention to Melissa since Iris had already had two cups of coffee.

Melissa ordered a low-fat candy apple latte. The green apple & cinnamon syrup was the perfect combination to satisfy her never ending sweet tooth. In addition, she added an apple tart to round off her selection. Next, Ina turned her attention to Iris who raised her hand, refusing any further offerings.

The ladies waited for Ina to step away from the table before starting their conversation. Melissa was the first to speak up.

"So, Iris, what has you so upset that you couldn't talk to me about it on the phone? You made it sound super urgent. My mind has been running wild since we hung up."

Iris closed her eyes and shook her head in disgust. "I told you it was a horrible idea for Christian to go to Tennessee. I felt it in my gut that it would not turn out well."

Melissa's forehead wrinkled, concern was etched across her face. "My goodness, what happened to Christian? I thought he was supposed to be home yesterday. Is he sick, or hurt?"

"Oh no, it's much worse than that. He brought back some country bumpkin with him. What's worse is he said she's his wife."

"His what?" Melissa asked, matching her tone.

"You heard me."

Ina returned to the table and quickly placed Melissa's order in front of her. Without waiting for further instruction, she stepped away, leaving the ladies alone. She knew it wasn't wise to stick around. Iris could be all out rude when she wanted to. Ina was determined to stay out of her crosshairs.

Melissa took a sip from her latte and moaned in delight. "Ooh, that's perfect. So Iris, who is this woman? I don't recall you ever saying he was engaged."

"He *wasn't* engaged," Iris snapped. "Apparently, it was a spur of the moment thing and they eloped yesterday morning before they flew back to L.A. That's not the worst

part. He didn't have her sign a prenup, and he had the nerve to get upset when I suggested he get a postnuptial agreement."

"No way. This doesn't sound like Christian at all. But I have to ask, what's so wrong with the woman that you are this upset?"

"Honey, let me tell you. I am the weed eater and this girl is definitely a weed. She's got to go."

"What are you going to do? I can't imagine you taking this laying down." Melissa nibbled on her tart while waiting on Iris to respond.

"You've got that right. I'll have to make calculated steps because Christian has his head so far up this woman's behind that he can't think straight." Iris shook her head in disgust. "You mark my words, I will get rid of her, if it's the last thing that I do."

"Okay, now you're scaring me. Why is this affecting you so badly? You sound as though he did something against you personally. What's really going on? You are far too bothered by this."

Iris looked at Melissa as if she had lost her mind. She couldn't believe her friend would have the nerve to make such a statement. Melissa should have known how much Christian meant to Iris. They had been friends for over 20 years and during that time Iris always made Christian her main priority.

"I'm not in the mood for one of your jokes today, Melissa. This is serious," Iris replied, issuing a strong rebuke to her friend.

She picked up a cloth napkin and began wringing it, as if it were filled with water. With sadness in her eyes, she stated barely above a whisper, "What happened to the man I raised? I don't even recognize this person. My son would never have pulled a stunt like this. They must have put some kind of hex on him or something. I'm telling you, I don't trust that woman, Melissa."

"Surely not, Iris." Melissa was careful to not upset her friend any further. "Just give it some time. Everything will work out, you'll see. If she's not right for him, he will see it and get rid of her. Christian is a very smart man, and you raised him right. He'll come around."

Iris opened her mouth to protest when her breath caught in her throat. Walking in her direction was the most handsome man she had seen in a very long time. His sun-kissed ebony skin was partially concealed by a fitted charcoal gray suit that struggled to keep his muscular frame at bay. If she had to guess, she'd say he stood just shy of six feet in stature, which would complement her five feet eight-inch frame nicely. He stepped towards her, and for a moment his chestnut brown eyes made contact with hers, causing her hair to seemingly stand on end. As he glided past her, he left behind a tantalizing spicy woody aroma that put the coffee house to shame. She imagined running her fingers through his wavy, cropped, salt and pepper gray hair that faded nicely into his beard and goatee.

"Iris!" Melissa exclaimed, snapping her fingers in front of Iris' face.

"What?" Iris snapped back, upset that Melissa had pulled her from her moment of fantasy.

"You sure did get over being mad awful fast."

"Girl, please. A man like that will make you forget your own name. Besides, there's nothing wrong with a little eye candy."

"Honey, with the way you're acting, I'd say that candy sent you straight into a diabetic coma."

Iris looked at her friend and couldn't help but to laugh. It had been a long time since a man captured her attention the way the handsome stranger had. Any man that could capture her attention like that was worth getting to know.

Five

Shelby sat behind the large polished oak desk in the home office and stared at the computer monitor. She scrolled through web page after web page hoping to find something that would capture her attention. She had only been in Los Angeles for a week, but she was already bored out of her mind. She pulled air into her lungs and expelled it with an exaggerated exhale. With five weeks left before she would start classes at the Fashion Institute to become a Fashion Stylist, her frustration with being stuck in the house was mounting. She knew she would miss her friends and family in Tennessee when she moved away, but she never imagined the separation would be this hard. The two-hour time difference made communicating difficult, and to top it all off she was still experiencing the remnants of jet-lag. Leaning forward, she rested her head in her left hand while keeping her right hand glued to the mouse, clicking aimlessly on the images on the screen.

Her phone rang and vibrated simultaneously, awakening her from her virtual coma. Quickly glancing at the display, she allowed a smile to gently part her lips as an image of Christian and the title *Husband* appeared on the screen. Sliding her manicured finger across the front of the phone, she answered in her most sensual tone.

"Hello, husband."

"Um hmm, I like the sound of that, girl. You almost made me forget I was at work."

"Yeah, right. I just bet I did."

"You think I'm playing, but it's a good thing I'm in this office alone and sitting down because if I wasn't I'd have some explaining to do."

Shelby burst into laughter. "Shame on you, Mr. Tyler."

Christian's laughter mingled with hers. "I guarantee you I'm not lying. Hey, I'm a newlywed. It's supposed to be like this. As good as you've been to me this week, just the thought of you puts a smile on my face."

"You better be careful, Blake is gonna take your playa card if he hears you talking like that," Shelby teased.

"Nah, baby. When I married you, I gladly surrendered it. As a matter of fact, after Blake met you he told me he didn't blame me for giving it up."

Christian chose to eliminate the part of his conversation with his best friend when Blake declared he needed to go to Tennessee and grab him a southern chick with a cornbread booty. He figured she wouldn't appreciate that part.

"Now I know you didn't call me to talk about Blake, so what's up?"

"Actually, I called to tell you we've been invited to a dinner party next week. The executives of Rising Star Studios are hosting a party in celebration of the upcoming project and they have asked me to attend. You know I'll need my favorite girl by my side. I can't wait to show you off."

"Oh, my God!" Shelby shrieked into the phone, causing Christian to quickly pull the phone away from his ear. "What am I going to wear?"

"Don't even worry about that, I've got you covered. I

gave Shantrice the afternoon off. She's gonna come by and pick you up in about an hour. I figured since you're new here, you wouldn't mind having her tag along to show you where the best shops are.

"Thank you, Christian. Thank you so much. I have to get off this phone. If I'm going shopping in L.A. I need to get ready."

"Enjoy yourself. While you're out shopping, get a little something for me."

~~ → ~~

Shelby ended her call with Christian and quickly dashed up the stairs to get dressed. Since moving to L.A. she had spent most of her days at home familiarizing herself with her new surroundings. With the exception of a couple of dinners out with Christian, she hadn't taken any time to explore her new city. Shelby was glad Shantrice would be accompanying her on her shopping excursion. It would be like having a personal tour guide.

Stepping into her room sized walk-in closet, Shelby walked over to the area where her clothes were hanging, perfectly organized by color and type. She selected a pair of light blue denim skinny jeans, and a coral, off the shoulder top that tied at the waist on her left side. She finished the look with a pair of patent leather coral pumps. Finally, she added a few large curls to her hair and pulled the tresses over to one side, securing the look with Bobbie pins.

The doorbell rang and Shelby hurried to the door. Shantrice stood at the door with a huge grin, holding Christian's credit card up for Shelby to clearly see.

"What do you say we get our Betty and Wilma Flintstone

on and charge it?" Shantrice said, laughing at her own joke.

Shelby took the card from her hand and followed Shantrice out to her white BMW M3 convertible. Once she was securely fastened in the seat, she examined the credit card. She had often heard about the quote unquote Black Card, but she never imagined actually holding one in her hand. She didn't want to show too much enthusiasm, especially since Christian's mother had already implied she was only interested in Christian because of his financial status. She hated that she had to prove her love for her husband to outsiders.

She ran her fingers across the card number and flinched. "Shantrice, wait," she urged. "This card doesn't have my name on it."

"Oh, don't worry, it's fine. He made you an authorized user, so there won't be a problem. Now let's go get our shop on."

Laughing, Shelby leaned against the back of the seat and said, "Let's do it."

Shantrice cruised through the streets of L.A., pointing out landmarks as she drove. The weather was a perfect seventy-three degrees. She drove as carefully as she could while keeping up with the busy traffic.

Shelby tried not to appear too touristy, but she was overjoyed with the sights and sounds of the city. She was tempted to go on the Hollywood Walk of Fame, but that was something she wanted to experience with Christian by her side.

"The dinner party you and Mr. Tyler are attending is formal. We're going to find you an exquisite gown worthy of your debut appearance as an elite Los Angeles socialite. I was also told you weren't able to bring very many of your

clothes since your move was so swift. I was told to make sure you got whatever you want to make you feel comfortable and at home."

Shantrice approached the mall and saw Shelby's eyes widen with delight.

"Wow, this is a beautiful mall," Shelby declared. She admired the curved architecture and the lush palm trees strategically placed around the building.

"Welcome to the Beverly Center," Shantrice announced. "You should be able to find pretty much anything you're looking for here. They have just about every high-end store you can imagine, Prada, Louis Vuitton, Saint Laurent, you name it. It's likely here."

"That sounds awesome, but I can't let Christian spend that kind of money on me. That's not why I married him."

Shantrice pulled into the parking garage located off Beverly Boulevard. Choosing to self-park rather than use the valet, she drove throughout the lot searching for the first available slot. She threw on brakes when she noticed a car backing out of a spot near the entrance close to Bloomingdales. Turning her steering wheel with precision, she quickly secured the available slot. She turned and looked at Shelby with the compassion of a dear friend. "Look, Shelby, I know you and I don't know each other very well, but I do know Mr. Tyler. He wouldn't have sent me to get you and given me the card to give to you if he didn't feel like you needed or deserved it. Now, how you choose to spend the money is up to you. This mall has Express and H&M inside as well. Please hear me when I say this. He loves you and he knows you love him. I can tell you right now, that man is going to try to give you the world so you may as well get used to it."

Shelby considered her words. She knew Shantrice was right. It had always been her dream to have a man that would love her and desire to give her the world. She loved Christian and although her initial desire when she first saw him was to see what she could get from him, that quickly faded once she got to know him. She wanted to be a woman he could be proud of and want to show off. It was time for her to let go of her inhibitions and enjoy being Mrs. Shelby Tyler.

At this moment, Shelby missed Kim and Dominique more than ever. She knew if her girls were with her there was no way she would need all the convincing Shantrice had to do. Kim would have popped her upside her head, snatched the card out of her hand, and ran into the mall.

"Alright, Shantrice, let's go and make me into a California girl." Shelby pulled on the door handle, and exited the vehicle.

Shelby stepped inside the mall and knew she was no longer in small town, Tennessee. The appearance of the mall caused butterflies to dance in her belly. She admired the décor of modern designed chairs and couches, seating she had never seen in a mall back home. It looked more like a tech genius' living room than a mall. The bright white ceiling, chandeliers, and huge circular skylights gave the mall interior a sci-fi appearance.

"Girl, how many floors does this mall have? This place is huge."

"It's eight levels," Shantrice answered nonchalantly.

"Eight!" Shelby exclaimed, looking down at her feet. "I wore the wrong shoes."

"You know what, I didn't even think to look at your

shoes when I picked you up. Although they're cute, those definitely will not work," Shantrice replied, pointing at the coral pumps with the three-inch stiletto heel.

"I guess that makes choosing our first store a little easier." Shelby let out a slight chuckle as she headed in the direction of the nearest shoe store.

After donning a fresh pair of sole babies, as Shelby liked to refer to her shoe collection, she was ready for her shopping spree. It didn't take her long to get over her reservations of spending a large amount of money. Three hours of shopping left both Shelby and Shantrice exhausted. They headed toward the nearest seating and relaxed.

"I don't know about you, but I have worked up a nice little appetite," Shantrice said, patting her belly."

"I'm with you," Shelby agreed. "I can definitely go for a bite. What do you say we conclude this trip and go grab a bite to eat? It's on me," she said, smiling broadly.

"It looks like it's on my son."

Shelby snapped her head around to find, Iris standing over her shoulder.

"Excuse me?" she replied, clearly offended.

"There is no excuse for you," Iris barked, sneering at shopping bags littered around Shelby's feet.

Shantrice quickly glanced at Shelby and Iris before turning her head. She pulled her phone from her pocket and sent Christian a text message.

Mayday! At the mall with Shelby, your mom's here. She's not happy.

Not this again... Christian texted back, immediately.

Yeah, Shelby looks embarrassed. I feel sorry for her.

Let me know if it escalates. Shelby can hold her own so I'm not too worried.

Will do. Shantrice returned her phone to her pocket and watched the ladies' interaction.

"It's nice to see you too, Ms. Tyler. You're looking well." Shelby addressed her mother-in- law as if she hadn't just insulted her.

"Humph. Look at you. You haven't been here two weeks and you're already trying to run my son into the poor house."

"I'm sorry you feel that way, as that is clearly not the case. Hopefully, you'll soon get to know me and find out I'm not the person you believe I am. I love Christian and I want the best for him, just as you do. Now if you will excuse me, we were on our way out."

Shelby gathered her shopping bags and stepped around Iris. Shantrice rose quickly and caught up to Shelby who was already several steps ahead.

Neither Shantrice nor Shelby spoke until they were secure inside Shantrice's vehicle. Shelby was the first to speak up as Shantrice exited the parking lot.

"That woman gets on my nerves so bad. Had I known I would have to go through all this drama I would have stayed in Bethany. My own mother doesn't talk to me like that. Christian better get his mama, I ain't even playing."

"I can imagine it's difficult enough being here away from your friends and family, and not really knowing anybody. I'm sorry you're having to deal with this. I'm sure Miss Tyler will come around. Just give her a little time."

Shelby rolled her eyes and stared out the window. All of the enjoyment she had from the shopping trip seemed to dissipate the moment Iris Tyler showed up.

"Don't let this ruin your day, Shelby. You bought some beautiful clothes and shoes, and most importantly you purchased your gown for the dinner party. Now, I don't know about you, but I'm starved. There's a great restaurant a few blocks away. What do you say we go ahead and grab a

bite?" Shantrice looked at Shelby with a pleading expression. Although she didn't agree with Iris' tactics, she was not going to speak against the mother of her employer to his wife, of all people.

Surrendering, Shelby threw her hands in the air, leaned against the seat and replied, "Alright let's go." *This isn't over, Iris Tyler. I see I'll have to show you who I am.*

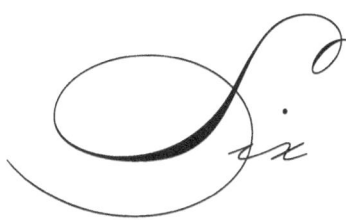

"Girl, I told you, that woman is after my son's money," Iris yelled into the phone.

"Wait a minute, Iris. What's going on, and why are you yelling?" Melissa replied, matching Iris' tone.

"I just left the Beverly Center and who do I see with so many bags that she could barely carry them, that hussy."

"Nooo. Already?"

"Yes, and she had the nerve to have Christian's assistant with her. I'll admit that was pretty surprising since Shantrice has always had my son's back in the past. I guess you never really know people."

"I'd hate to jump to conclusions, Iris, but I will admit, that looks pretty bad. She's only been here a couple of weeks based on what you've told me. Maybe it was her own money."

"Are you being serious right now? Of course, it wasn't her money. I see I'll have to step up my efforts. This cannot and will not continue. At least not on my watch, and I don't plan on going anywhere. I'll talk to you later."

Iris disconnected the call before Melissa could go into her optimistic mumbo jumbo. She was Iris' best friend, but she could really work her nerves at times. She was always trying to see the so called good in people. Iris on the other hand took people at face value and more times than not, she

31

was right. It was time Iris paid her son a visit. She wouldn't dare go back to the home he had practically banned her from. This time she was going to the one place where she knew Shelby wouldn't be.

"Hello, Mother," Christian said, stepping away from his desk. He approached Iris and offered her a hug.

"Son, what are you doing?"

"What do you mean? I'm working." Christian knew exactly what his mother was talking about, but he was content on playing ignorant.

"I just left the Beverly Center and I saw that woman and your assistant. She had so many bags, it looked like she tried to hit every high-end store in the mall. I know she's from back woods Tennessee and has probably never seen quality clothes but this is ridiculous." Iris placed her purse on the edge of his desk and took a seat in one of the two chairs adjacent to his desk.

Christian released an audible sigh. He was happy Shantrice had warned him while she and Shelby were at the mall. He walked behind his desk and took a seat, placed his elbows on the desk, and folded his hands. He was growing tired of explaining his marriage and defending his wife to his mother.

"Mother, did it ever occur to you that perhaps Shelby has money of her own? You have judged her from the moment I introduced the two of you. It's very disappointing. I can understand your being upset over not knowing Shelby prior to our marriage. I realize I disappointed you and I'm honestly sorry for that, but this has to stop."

Iris sat up in the chair ready for combat.

Christian raised his palms in an effort to calm his mother down. "Wait a minute, Mother. Please hear me out.

Shelby is very successful in her own right. She owns a home in Bethany. She has her own vehicle, and before you ask, yes, it's paid for. Not only that, she has a very promising career in the fashion industry. Shelby was accepted into The Fashion Institute prior to coming here. She starts school in a couple of weeks. So, you see, you and her have a few things in common."

"Humph. I suppose that's good for her. However, I stand by my opinion. Just because you think you love her doesn't mean she's right for you. We went through this before with Alexia. I warned you about her and I was right."

"Yes, you were right about Alexia, but I'm telling you, Shelby is not like that. You'll see. Now, if you don't mind, I'd rather not talk about this any further." Christian reached over to a glass tray on his desk and retrieved a small envelope. He pulled out the note card and passed it over to his mother.

"The executives for Rising Star Studios are hosting a dinner party to celebrate the new expansion. I would love for you to be there."

Iris studied the invitation intently. "This says plus one. Seeing as though you're inviting me, I hope this means you're taking me and leaving her at home."

"No, Mother. I have already had Shantrice to inform them that I will be bringing two guests. Your name has been added to the guest list, due to the fact that we will be arriving separately. It's going to be fun and I want you there."

"Fine," she said, surrendering. Iris had never been one to pass up a social event, and she wasn't about to start. She pulled out her phone and entered the information into her calendar.

~~∂~~

The night of the dinner party had arrived and Shelby was ready to step out for her first social event with her husband. She had spent the day getting her hair and nails done at Camera Ready Salon in Antioch. Shantrice recommended the salon after Shelby expressed a need to get her hair and nails ready for the event. Shelby hated having to depend on Shantrice so much, but she didn't have much choice, being new to the area.

Christian walked over to his bedside table and retrieved his keys and cellphone. The stylish black slim-fit suit he wore was perfect for the occasion. He wasn't overdressed nor was he under dressed.

"Are you ready, babe?" Christian called out to Shelby who was still in her walk-in closet and dressing room.

"Just about, I'll be out in a minute," Shelby replied as she stood in front of the mirror, applying the final touches of her makeup.

"I'm going to grab something to drink while you finish up. I'll meet you downstairs."

"Okay, I'll be right down."

Shelby examined her appearance in the full length mirror. She was confident that she had nailed the look she was going for. The true test would come when Christian laid eyes on her. If she received the reaction she was expecting, she'd know she had succeeded.

Christian walked out of the kitchen with a bottle of Coke to his lips when he heard Shelby walking down the stairs. Just as he was turning up the bottle he stopped and stared at her. He rushed to place the bottle on a round glass table located in the foyer, before approaching his wife.

He reached for her hand and helped her down the remaining two stairs. "You are a vision of beauty, my love.

I'm tempted to forget the party, and take you back upstairs."

"Christian, you are a mess. You're looking pretty spiffy yourself. Besides, as much time as I spent preparing for tonight and getting ready, we are going to that party."

"Ooh girl, you look good. That dress looks like it was designed especially for you." Christian raised Shelby's hand in the air and turned her a full three hundred sixty degrees, taking in every inch of her. The ankle length, candy apple red, off the shoulder gown she was wearing hugged her in all the right places. A high split teased him, allowing her thigh to be exposed as she walked. Finally, he rested his eyes on the sweetheart neckline that allowed the sparkling body oil to dance on top of her cleavage "Umm, ummm, ummm. I am one blessed man," he said before allowing a low whistle to escape his lips.

Shelby let out a soft giggle. *Mission accomplished,* she thought.

"Shall we, Mrs. Tyler?" Christian extended his arm to Shelby.

"We shall, Mr. Tyler," Shelby replied, taking Christian's arm and matching his stride.

Christian leaned over and placed a light kiss on her lips as they headed out the door.

Shelby stared in amazement at the enormous and brightly lit estate as Christian pulled his jet-black Bentley Continental GT around the circular driveway to the awaiting valet. Two men dressed in red vests approached the car on either side and opened the doors to allow Christian and Shelby to exit the vehicle. Christian quickly walked around the car and placed his hand on the small of Shelby's back.

"Wow, this place is huge," Shelby whispered in awe.

"Yeah, I know. It's at least twenty thousand square feet. I guess you can ball like that when you own a major motion picture studio. The uplighting that surrounded the tan brick structure gave it an appearance similar to a Las Vegas hotel. Huge windows were placed along the front of the three story mansion. The windows on the second floor each had a small black wrought iron balcony.

Guests were greeted by butlers dressed in black tuxedos with crisp tails. Starched white shirts and black bowties completed their look. Upon entrance into the foyer, Shelby looked up and noticed a large crystal chandelier. She gasped when she saw a replica of Michelangelo's painting, The Creation of Adam, on the ceiling. Gold banisters extended the length of the stairs leading up to the second floor. A second set of butlers escorted guests into a ballroom located to the left of the foyer. A full staff of servers, dressed in white shirts with black bowties and black slacks, moved easily among the crowd carrying trays that contained flutes of champagne, and various hors d'oeuvres.

"Christian, my man, I'm glad you could make it." Vincent Garrett greeted Christian with a firm hand shake. Turning to Shelby he asked, "And who do we have here?"

Smiling, Christian pulled his wife closer to him and said, "This is my beautiful wife, Shelby."

"Oh, I didn't realize you were married." Vincent extended his hand to Shelby.

"We're newlyweds," Christian said, placing a light kiss on Shelby's ear.

Holding his hands up in surrender, Vincent chuckled. "Don't worry, Christian, you have nothing to worry about

with me. Anyone that looks at the two of you can tell you're in love. I've experienced that kind of love before with my late wife. I'm confident I'll have it again one day when the man upstairs sees fit to bless me. Congratulations to the both of you."

Vincent continued to chat with Christian and Shelby. He spoke with them about his home, and about his excitement over the studio expansion they were preparing to begin in a couple of weeks. They were all so engaged in conversation that neither noticed the woman approaching them.

Iris entered the ballroom wearing an elegant silver, half sleeved gown. The lights reflected off her beaded lace appliques giving her a glowing appearance. She saw Christian and Shelby speaking to a man with salt and pepper gray hair wearing a black tuxedo. She moved through the crowd until she was standing next to them.

"Mom, you made it," Christian said, releasing Shelby and pulling Iris into a warm embrace. "Mr. Garrett, this is my mother, Iris Tyler. Mom, this is Vincent Garrett, the owner of Rising Star Studios."

"It's a pleasure to meet you, Mrs. Tyler," Vincent said, extending his hand to Iris and flashing a smile that was destined to melt her heart."

"Thank you, but it's Miss Tyler," Iris replied, accepting his hand and returning the smile. She could barely find her voice. Standing in front of her holding her hand was the man that left her speechless when she and Melissa were at the coffee shop.

"That's good to know," Vincent said, still holding on to Iris. "I feel like we've met somewhere before."

"We haven't met officially. I saw you at a coffee shop a couple of weeks ago."

"Yeah, the coffee shop. I remember," Vincent replied, increasing the bass in his voice.

Christian and Shelby looked at each other and then back at Iris and Vincent. Christian cleared his throat to remind Iris and Vincent that he and Shelby were still present.

Shelby elbowed Christian in his side. The attraction between Vincent and Iris was obvious. She didn't want anything or anyone to interfere. The thought of Iris having her own man excited Shelby. She figured that was the key to getting Iris to butt out of her and Christian's marriage.

Vincent released Iris' hand. "Excuse me, I better make my rounds before my other guests start to feel neglected. Please enjoy the party."

Iris watched as Vincent stepped away. She couldn't believe she was in the home of the man that she hadn't stopped thinking about from the moment she'd first laid eyes on him.

Christian mingled among the crowd, introducing his wife and mother to some of the other guests. A ten piece orchestra played classic tunes throughout the evening.

Hours after their initial meeting, Vincent hadn't returned to speak with them any further. Noting the time, Iris excused herself from the party. She embraced Christian and offered a flat smile to Shelby.

"I'm going to get out of here," Iris stated, directing her full attention to Christian.

"Wait, Mom. It is getting pretty late. Shelby and I should probably call it a night as well."

"No, you stay. I don't want you to leave on my account. Enjoy yourselves, I'll speak with you tomorrow."

Iris turned and made her exit. She hated she didn't get to see Vincent anymore. She was still relishing in the warmth of his hand holding hers. *Lord, I'm getting too old for this puppy love stuff*, she thought. Although she had to admit the thought of having a man in her life was quite appealing. She handed her ticket to the valet and pulled out her phone to text Melissa while she waited for her car.

"You're leaving so soon?" A sexy male voice asked just above a whisper.

Iris turned to find Vincent standing behind her. His scent was intoxicating. She didn't know how long she had stood in silence, but she figured it must have been a moment too long because she heard Vincent calling her name."

Giggling, more out of embarrassment than anything, Iris found her voice. "Yes, I'm heading home. It was a lovely party. Thank you for having me.

"The pleasure was all mine. In fact, I'd hate to leave things up to chance. I would love to see you again, with a much smaller crowd. Will you allow me to perhaps take you to dinner sometime?"

"That would be nice," Iris replied.

Vincent slipped her phone out of her hands and pulled up the dial pad. He entered his phone number and pressed the call button before placing the phone back in her hand. His phone vibrated in his jacket pocket indicating the call coming in. "Now, all you have to do is save my number, so that you'll know it's me when I call."

"In that case, I'll look forward to your call," Iris replied as the valet pulled up in her glacier white Audi S5 Cabriolet. He stepped out of the car, allowing her room to climb inside.

Vincent watched her drive away before returning inside to the party.

Iris pressed the hands free button with her thumb as she applied a firm grip to the steering wheel. This call could not wait until morning. She waited with much impatience until the call connected.

"Hello."

"Oh, my God, you will not believe who I just saw," she yelled into the microphone implanted in her rearview mirror.

"Who?" Melissa asked, matching Iris' excitement.

"The man from the coffee shop."

"Coffee shop? What coffee shop?" Melissa asked.

"We only go to one, Melissa. I know you remember, think about it."

"Oh!" Melissa exclaimed. "You're talking about the man that left you speechless when you were in the middle of fussing about Christian and his wife."

"Yes, girl. That's the one."

"Where did you see him?"

"I saw him this evening at the dinner party Christian invited me to. His name is Vincent Garrett. Turns out he owns Rising Star Studios, the company Christian recently received the huge contract for."

"I cannot believe it," Melissa said, expressing excitement for her best friend.

"If you can't believe that, then you're really not going to believe this. Girl, I had pulled out my phone to text you while I waited for my car and he approached me from behind. He told me he would like to have dinner with me right before he took my phone out of my hands and put in his number."

"Girl, stop. He gave you his number? Do you know how rich that man is?"

"I found that out when I went to his house where the party was held. When he shook my hand, he refused to let it go. But, beyond that, do you remember how fine he was? I can't wait for him to call me."

"I know you can't. I'm happy for you, bestie."

Iris took a deep breath. "Look at me sitting here acting like some teenaged girl. Let me get myself together."

"Don't you dare start, Iris."

"Start what?"

"You do this every time. You always find a way to turn something good into a negative."

"No, I don't. I'm just a realist. I call things like they are. You know I've dated wealthy men before. The problem with these guys is they always seem to view you like you're another piece of property, and as such they don't treat you the best. Most of the wealthy men I've dated acted as though they were doing me a favor and that I should be grateful that they were dating me. On top of that, being faithful was not their strong suit."

"Every man is not like that, Iris. I know you've been hurt a lot in your past. But hey, don't count this guy out without at least having dinner with him first. It can't be a coincidence that you saw him at the coffee shop and went absolutely crazy over him, and then ended up at his house. That has to count for something."

Iris arrived home and pulled into her garage. "Perhaps you're right. Now the other thing is I don't know how he'll feel about me living in Inglewood."

"Oh, now you want to think about it. Christian has tried to get you to move for years, but you weren't having it." Melissa chuckled. "If he's truly a good guy, it won't even matter. Now let me get off this phone. Dean is waiting for me in the other room."

"Don't you keep that man waiting. I'll talk to you tomorrow."

"Bye, girl," Melissa replied with a tone of mischief.

The ladies ended the call and Iris exited her vehicle. She stepped inside her modest three bedroom house and kicked off her shoes. She laid her purse and keys on the kitchen counter and made her way to her guest room turned walk-in closet. Iris took her time removing her gown and imagined what it would be like to have a man to share her life with. She hadn't thought about having a real relationship in years. Dating on occasion had been enough for her because she always had her son to fill in any feelings of loneliness. Now that he was married, she was forced to see herself as more than just Christian's mother. Involuntary tears stained her face. Without any input from her, Iris' life had changed and she had no control over it.

Turning to a mirror that sat in the corner of the room, Iris studied her features. She was still an attractive woman, despite the years that had passed. Her gray strands added a show of maturity without compromising her beauty. She hugged herself tightly and silently praised her well-kept figure. Fitness was a major part of her life and it showed.

"Well, Iris, a new day begins," she spoke to herself aloud before turning off the light and leaving the room.

The chime of her cell phone drew her attention back to the kitchen where she had left her iPhone.

You looked radiant tonight. I'm looking forward to seeing you again. Vincent texted.

Thank you. You were quite handsome yourself. She replied too quickly in her opinion. She didn't want to seem anxious.

You're too kind. Rest well pretty lady.

You too.

Iris danced from the kitchen to her bedroom, forgetting the sadness she had just experienced. Vincent Garrett was pursuing her and she was ready to be caught.

~~☙~~

"Did you see how Vincent was ogling my mother?" Christian asked as he paced the length of their bedroom. He loosened and snatched his bowtie off before slamming it onto his bedside table. "I can only imagine what he would have tried had we not been there."

"Christian, you have to calm down," Shelby urged, catching up to Christian and turning him to face her. "Mr. Garrett was a complete gentleman. Don't you see this is a good thing. You and I have found happiness in each other. Your mother deserves the same. Besides, he is quite handsome and super rich. Huh, I say go, Iris go."

"Don't make fun, Shelby."

"Who's making fun. I'm dead serious. If it was my mama I would be jumping up and down right now. I've been praying that God would send my mother someone for a long time. Instead of getting in your feelings, you should happy for her."

"Yeah, okay," Christian said with an air of defiance. He stepped away from Shelby and sat on the bed.

44

"You know what, this has been a great night. One that dreams are made of. I made some great connections with people that worked in both the fashion and motion picture industry. Instead of exhausting your energy moping around about your mother, how about you come and help me out of this dress. There's a surprise for you underneath."

Christian tried to stay angry, but his wife's sensual tone and soft touch caused his body to betray him.

Shelby looked down and smirked. "I see not all of you is angry. Now come and help me take this dress off."

With swift motions, Christian was standing next to his wife. He turned Shelby away from him and planted kisses on her exposed neck. Next, he unzipped her dress and allowed it to fall to the floor before consuming her with all of his passion.

Eight

"Hey, girl. What are you up to?" Melissa asked before Iris could utter hello.

"Hello to you too, Melissa. You're awfully perky this morning. How many cups of coffee have you had?"

"Honey, I don't know what you're talking about. I feel good. I had a restful sleep, and the sun is so beautiful this morning, it just makes you feel good. So, again I ask, what are you up to?"

"I'm folding clothes. I've been gathering them all morning for the Abigail Club clothing drive. Christian asked me to introduce little Miss Thang to the club. He said he wants her to get out more. I personally wouldn't care if she never got out."

"Be nice, Iris."

"I'm only being honest," Iris said, smacking her lips. "Besides, she's supposed to start school or something soon, anyway. I shouldn't have to be bothered with her. But, I love my son, so I'm willing to make the sacrifice."

"All right, enough about them, did he call yet?"

"Did who call?"

"Iris, don't play with me. You know exactly who I'm talking about. Did Vincent Garrett call?"

"Why do you have to say his full name? You could have simply said Vincent, but no, you have to be all dramatic. No, he has not called, and I'm not holding my breath waiting on a call either."

"He'll call, and when he does, don't be acting all snooty. You know you can do that sometimes." Melissa enjoyed teasing her friend. She knew just how to get under her skin.

"If he calls, you'll be the first to know. Now, if you don't mind, I need to get back to the task at hand. These clothes are not going to fold themselves."

"Alright, fine. I'm headed to the gym. Have fun with your daughter-in-law." Melissa disconnected the call, leaving the sound of laughter in Iris' ear.

"Ugh, she gets on my nerves," Iris declared aloud, tossing her phone on the bed. She resumed folding clothes and organizing her clothing donation. She made it a point to include a few new pieces along with the gently used items she was donating. Iris looked forward to the clothing drive held twice a year by the Abigail Club. There were so many men and women that moved to Los Angeles with dreams of stardom. All too often, many of the hopefuls found themselves struggling, completely broke, and in worse cases, homeless. The clothing drive helped the people tremendously.

Christian had caught her completely off guard when he asked her to involve Shelby in the event. She clearly didn't care for Shelby, and she was pretty sure the feeling was mutual. Iris wasn't sure what Christian's expectations were. Did he expect her and Shelby to ride together? Was she expected to take Shelby to each member and personally introduce her? The more Iris thought about it, the more frustrated she became. Who was Christian to dictate her life. She was the parent, not the other way around.

Hi Mom, Shelby is looking forward to going with you today. What time will you be by to pick her up?

"Ugh," Iris groaned after reading the message. She wanted to toss her phone to the other side of the room, but decided against it. Not only was she going to have to see the little twit today, but Christian expected them to ride together. That meant she would be stuck in the car with her, with no way of escape. The next thing you know he would be expecting them to talk or hang out together.

Fine, tell her I'll be there in a couple of hours. I need to finish up some things first.

K, Christian texted back.

Iris grabbed a large box she had been saving for the occasion and filled it with her donation. Like it or not, she was going to be stuck with Shelby for the next several hours. She loaded up the car and headed out. She had a few errands to run and she didn't want to wait until Shelby was with her to do them.

True to her word, Iris arrived at Christian's house exactly two hours after she told him she was coming. She could think of a ton of people other than Shelby that she would rather spend her Saturday with. But, she promised her son she would get to know his wife and now here she was stuck with her. She beeped the horn and waited for Shelby to come out.

Christian stepped out of the door carrying a large tote, followed by Shelby. Iris pushed the button to open the trunk so that Christian could place the tote inside. He then opened the door for Shelby to get in the car before finally making his way around to Iris' side.

"Hi, Ms. Tyler," Shelby said after she sat in the car."

"Hi, Shelby."

Christian pulled the driver side door open, and embraced his mother. "How're you doing, Mom?"

"Hello, son," Iris said dryly. Normally, she was happy to see her son, but she didn't like having Shelby shoved down her throat. She patted Christian on his back. "We better get going," she said, giving him a hint to let her go.

"Oh, of course," he replied, pulling back. "You girls have a good time."

Without a word, Iris put the car in gear and pulled away. They rode a couple of blocks in awkward silence. Iris decided to break the ice. They were going to spend several hours together and she didn't want the other volunteers to pick up on their tension. She had an image to uphold and she was not going to let Shelby interfere with that.

"How are you today, Shelby?"

Shelby was staring out of the window. She jumped, startled by Iris' attempt at conversation. "I'm doing well, thank you."

"I hope you don't mind working. This event is always very busy. It's a lot of hard work, and we don't have time for slackers."

"I'm no stranger to hard work. I'm looking forward to helping out. Thank you for inviting me," Shelby said.

Iris let out a "Humph." Shelby should have known better. There was no way that Iris would have invited her to do anything other than to hop on a plane back to Nowhere, Tennessee. If Christian lied about that, there was no telling how many more lies he had told concerning her. The sooner they got the day over with, the better. Iris wasn't going to spend any more time with Shelby than she had to.

They pulled up to the community center where the clothing drive would take place. People were already

forming a line near the entrance even though the event wouldn't start for another hour. Iris parked her car in the designated area where volunteers were waiting with carts to unload each donor's vehicle. She exited and waited for Shelby to get out before locking the doors.

"Follow me," she said walking ahead of Shelby into the building. As if someone had yelled action, Iris instantly turned on the charm, smiling and waving at fellow volunteers. A statuesque woman with a cropped curly afro approached them. She walked with elegance and a persona that commanded attention although she was dressed modestly in denim capris and a lavender V-neck tee. A stark contrast to Iris' St. Johns sequin knit top and satin pants.

"Winifred, how are you?" Iris asked, extending her arms to the woman. After a slight hug, they gave each other air kisses on each cheek. Winifred looked over at Shelby silently, prompting Iris for an introduction.

"This is Shelby, Christian's wife. She came to help us out today."

"Christian's what?" Winifred replied with a surprised expression.

"I know, it was a shock to us all," Iris said with dry sarcasm.

"It's very nice to meet you, Shelby. Thank you for coming. Lord knows we can use all the help we can get." The two ladies shook hands and Winifred excused herself.

Iris took Shelby around and introduced her to the other volunteers. Iris chose to help organize the donations while Shelby volunteered to help style the ladies and young girls. She helped them make outfits from the items they received.

As much as she hated to admit it, Iris acknowledged that Shelby was a natural stylist. She saw the expressions of joy the people had after Shelby had helped them. She treated them as if they were the rich and famous shopping at an exclusive boutique, instead of someone experiencing financial difficulties receiving donated clothes.

Not only did Iris notice Shelby, Winifred did also. "She's great at this," Winifred whispered to Iris as they stood around the refreshments table looking in Shelby's direction.

"Yes, she is," Iris replied. "The people seem to be happy, and that's what counts."

Winifred sat her cup down and turned to Iris. Her eyes beamed with excitement. "I have a great idea. Since you're always saying how overwhelmed you are chairing the fashion show fundraiser, why don't you ask Shelby to be your co-chair. Earlier when I went to check on her, she told me she was new to the area. The fashion show will give her the opportunity to meet some of our other members and benefactors."

"I'll ask her, but I can't be sure of her answer." Iris replied. "She'll be starting classes at the Fashion Institute soon, and it may be too much for her to do along with school."

"Let's find out." Winifred grabbed Iris by the hand and led her over to Shelby. They waited for Shelby to finish helping her current recipient before they approached her.

"You're going to look amazing in this outfit. Thank you for coming in today." Shelby gave the lady she was working with a hug. She turned and found Iris and Winifred staring at her.

"Shelby, you're doing an amazing job," Winifred said, beaming. "I've never seen so many smiles. I mean, the people are generally happy when they leave here but they seem a little more excited today. I believe it's because of the added attention that you are giving them. You're treating

them with so much dignity."

"It's my pleasure. I believe everyone deserves to be treated with dignity and respect. Besides, this is what I love to do. It's never work when you're doing what you love." Shelby let out a soft giggle.

"It certainly shows," Winifred said. Changing the subject, she continued, "Every year we host a fashion show fundraiser. Iris and I were thinking perhaps this year you could co-chair the event along with Iris. I know you have school starting soon, but if you could carve out any little bit of time to help, we would be ever so grateful."

Shelby looked over at Iris. Iris gave her a tight lipped smile and a slight nod. Seeing no objection or resistance from her mother-in-law, Shelby smiled at the ladies and answered, "I'd be delighted to help. Thank you so much for considering me."

Winifred pulled her into a big hug. "Wonderful. This is going to be amazing." She turned and hugged Iris. "Ladies, if you'll excuse me, I need to touch base with the other volunteers so that we can wrap things up. Thank you again for your help." She walked away, leaving Shelby and Iris behind.

"Thanks for considering me for the fundraiser, Ms. Tyler. I'm looking forward to helping you," Shelby said.

"Yeah," was Iris' only response. She started to walk away with Shelby trailing behind.

Iris laced up her running shoes and headed out the door. She was due to meet Melissa in twenty minutes at their favorite walking trail. They had a standing weekly commitment on Monday morning. When it rained, they went on the next dry day or they took their walk inside to the treadmills.

When Iris arrived at the park she found Melissa parked, eating an apple. She beeped her horn and waved at her best friend. Iris grabbed a bottle of water from her cup holder and jumped out of the car. She hadn't spoken to Melissa all weekend. She was bursting at the seams with all of the stuff she needed to tell her.

Melissa got out of her car and joined Iris for a light stretch before they started their walk. Iris opened her pedometer app on her phone before starting their two-mile trek. Melissa over exaggerated her arm movements, causing Iris to laugh.

"Girl, what are you doing?" Iris asked.

"I saw this online. They say it makes your heart pump faster and you get a better workout," Melissa replied.

"If you keep swinging like that you're going to wear yourself out, and I can't carry you back to your car when you pass out."

Melissa poked her lips out and relaxed her arms. "You

never want to try new stuff. You get on my nerves."

"We're too old to be trying new stuff."

"I beg to differ. You're never too old to try something new. Maybe if you try that man, Vincent, you won't be so crabby." She laughed.

"Ooh, no you didn't," Iris replied.

"Yes, I did and you should too."

Iris burst into laughter once again. Melissa was the only one that could talk to her like that and get away with it. "Girl, you are a mess. I'm not going there with you today. Anyway, I need to tell you about this past weekend."

"Oh yeah, the clothing drive. How did things go with your daughter-in-law?"

"You need to stop calling her that, Melissa."

"What am I supposed to call her? She *is* your daughter-in-law."

"You can call her Shelby. I'll know exactly who you're talking about. I'm going to surprise you when I tell you this."

"What?"

"Shelby actually did a great job at the clothing drive. She didn't embarrass me at all, which I am very surprised by. Christian told me she was going to school to be a fashion stylist and I could see that . She is gifted in that area for sure."

Melissa looked at Iris amazed. "Who are you and what have you done with my best friend? I can't believe you are giving her a compliment."

Iris took a sip from her water bottle. "I believe in giving credit where credit is due. She did a good job. So much so that Winifred asked her to co-chair the fashion show fundraiser."

"*Your* fashion show fundraiser?"

"Yep. That's the one."

"No. How do you feel about that? I mean that fashion show is your event. You've worked really hard to build that event up."

Iris considered her words. She had allowed Winifred's excitement over Shelby to cloud her judgment. "You know what, you're right. I can't seem to get away from this girl. I didn't want to take her with me to the clothing drive to begin with, and now I'm stuck with her for the fashion show. There's a lot of work involved in that show and I really don't feel like spending that much time with her."

"You've been saying you could use some help with it. I guess you got it now." Melissa laughed herself breathless.

"Forget you, Melissa. It's not that funny."

The ladies reached their one mile mark and stopped to catch their breath. They always enjoyed their time together and chose not to rush things. They started mile two heading back to their vehicles.

"Have you heard from Vincent yet?" Melissa asked.

"Vincent Garrett has not called me, and he probably won't. There were a lot of women at the dinner party that night. Not only that night, but I'm sure a rich, handsome man like Vincent has his pick of women. I'm not focusing my attention on him. I have plenty going on in my life to keep me busy."

Melissa crossed her arms and looked over her shoulder at her friend. "Say what you want, I believe he will call you, and when he does that tough exterior you keep trying to hide behind will crumble like a cookie made with margarine."

The ladies arrived back at their cars and performed another light stretch. Iris pulled out her phone to check her steps. "That little walk gave me 4200 steps. Not bad,

I guess." She was about to put the phone away when it started ringing. She looked at the name on the display and immediately turned to Melissa with her mouth open. "It's him," she mouthed afraid to speak too loudly as if he could hear her.

"Answer it," Melissa mouthed back.

Iris quickly pressed the accept button before the call went to voicemail. "Hello," she answered in her most sultry tone.

"Hello...Iris?" Vincent said as more of a question than a greeting. His sexy baritone sent a shiver down her spine.

"Yes, this is Iris."

"Iris, this is Vincent Garret. We met when you attended a dinner party at my home."

"I know who this is. You put your number in my phone, remember?"

"Of course I remember. I just didn't know if you kept it in your phone or deleted it. I'm glad to know you kept it. That means you were looking forward to my call."

"Is that right? No one can accuse you of lacking confidence."

"Sweetheart, I didn't get where I am today by not having confidence. Now that's enough about me. How are you this morning?"

Iris leaned up against her car. Melissa stood right beside her. She was so close she could hear both ends of the conversation. "I'm doing good. Just wrapping up my workout. How about you?"

"I'm good. I got my workout in this morning too. I'm glad to know you believe in keeping that body right."

Melissa dropped her bottle of water. Iris waved her hand to get her friend to behave. She stifled her laugh.

"I definitely believe in taking care of myself. You only get one body and one life. You have to take care of it. After all, if I don't take care of it, who will?"

"Do you really want me to answer that question?" Vincent asked.

Iris giggled. " I believe you just did." Her voice dripped with seduction.

Melissa twisted her lip and raised her hand in the air, snapping her fingers.

Vincent let out a slight chuckle. "I like how you think, Iris. I love a no nonsense woman. Let me get to the reason for my call. I told you I wanted to take you out sometime. I was wondering if you're available for lunch this afternoon."

"Hmmm, I should be available this afternoon. Say one o'clock?"

"One o'clock is good. Where would you like to meet?"

"Let's go to Perch on Hill Street. Would you like for me to pick you up?"

"Oh no, I'll meet you there.

"I don't mind coming to get you. It's not a problem."

"Perhaps after we become more acquainted with one another I'll let you pick me up. For now, I prefer to drive myself. I hope you understand."

"I understand completely, and I respect your decision. You agreed to have lunch. That's enough for me."

"I better go so that I can get ready. I'll see you shortly." Iris ended her call with Vincent and she was met with a high five from Melissa. They did a quick dance, followed by a hug.

"You better get out of here so that you can get ready. I can't wait to hear about your date."

They jumped in their vehicles and quickly left the park.

Iris drove in quiet anticipation. She didn't know what to expect, but she was optimistic. It had been a long time since she'd dated and as much as she hated to admit it, she felt a little rusty. She didn't want to mess things up by making a complete fool of herself. Above all, she hoped her opinion of him was accurate and that he wouldn't turn out to be a jerk.

Iris arrived at home and quickly showered. She felt like a giddy schoolgirl instead of the well-established, mature woman that she was. She hadn't had a man to cause her to react this way in years. After her shower, she went into her dressing room and scanned the racks. Her eyes fell on a teal, knee length, off the shoulder dress. She grabbed a pair of rose gold pumps and got dressed.

Traffic was horrible. Iris didn't think she would ever arrive at the restaurant. She pulled her car into a nearby parking lot and hopped out. Glancing down at her watch she saw she was ten minutes early. She walked the short distance to the Pershing Square building and headed inside.

After what felt like a short eternity of waiting, the elevator arrived and the door parted, allowing her access. Iris stepped inside and pressed the illuminated button for the fifteenth floor. Her mind raced with anticipation of her lunch date. Just as the doors were closing, she heard a voice call out.

"Hold the elevator!"

She quickly pressed the door's open button, halting the closure.

"Thank you, beautiful," a male voice said, pulling her back to the present. An immediate smile formed on her lips as she breathlessly took in the attractive towering figure.

"My pleasure," she said in a voice overflowing with sensuality. She didn't know what it was about Vincent

Garrett, but this man had a way of arousing her beyond anything she could imagine. Even in her younger years no man had ever made her feel the way he did.

Vincent reached down and grabbed her hand, pulling it to his lips. He kissed the inside of her palm with such gentleness that it caused her heart rate to multiply.

The elevator jerked a bit while coming to a halt. "I must say, you are wearing that dress." He bit on his bottom lip and turned her around in a full spin, taking in every inch of her. "Are you ready for lunch?" he asked, extending his arm to her as they exited the elevator.

"I sure am," Iris answered honestly.

"Today is such a beautiful day. I made our reservations for the patio," Vincent said. "What better way to see downtown Los Angeles on a day like today?"

"I agree, it *is* a beautiful day. The patio is fine."

The hostess showed them to their table and took their drink orders. Their server followed the hostess almost immediately. He introduced himself as Fabio causing Iris to snicker. The server's muscular build and long blond hair put her in the mind of the model from the 80s and 90s. They placed their orders and Fabio quickly stepped away from their table.

"I guess he is Fabio 2.0," Vincent said, causing Iris to release the laugh that she was trying so hard to stifle.

She stopped laughing when she noticed Vincent staring at her. She cleared her throat, and sat up straight in her chair, returning his gaze. "What?" she asked, trying to sound unfazed.

"You have a beautiful laugh. I was enjoying it. Why did you stop?"

"Because I felt a little awkward seeing as though you

weren't laughing with me. I felt like I was on my own," Iris admitted. She reached for her glass and took a sip.

"On the contrary, my dear. You don't ever have to worry about being on your own when you're with me. I'll always make sure you're well taken care of."

"Is that right?"

"You better believe it," Vincent answered. He raised his glass and reached over toward Iris. "What do you say we toast to new beginnings."

Tapping his glass with hers, Iris said, "I'd say, I'll drink to that."

They carried on light conversation while they waited on their food. They found out they had a lot in common. They both enjoyed family, fitness, and traveling to exotic places. Fabio returned, setting the plate of scallops in front of Iris before placing the bouillabaisse Vincent ordered in front of him, along with an empty bowl to collect the shells.

"This looks delicious," Iris said.

"The food here is amazing. I'm sure you'll enjoy it." Vincent scooped a spoonful of broth up and slurped it."

Iris gave him a very unflattering look, causing him to laugh.

"I'm just teasing you. I don't eat like that." They continued to enjoy easy conversation during their meal.

Iris was amazed at how easily she communicated with Vincent. She had a preconceived notion of how he would behave, given his economic status, but instead she found him to be just as down to earth and easy to communicate with as anyone else. She was careful to stay away from conversations that would lead to money or business. She was too old in her opinion to be viewed as a gold digger. She would leave that title up to Shelby.

Following their meal, Vincent paid and added a generous tip for Fabio before escorting Iris out of the restaurant. He walked her to her car and offered her a peck on the cheek. Once she slid inside, he pushed her door closed and tapped his hand on the door. Out of nowhere, he leaned in and planted a kiss on her lips. Iris returned the jester. Vincent backed away from the car so that she could back out of the parking slot.

She drove down the street feeling like she was floating on a cloud. Iris was determined to not fall too deeply into his grasp. After all, he was still the super-rich studio owner and although her son made sure she was very well taken care of, she didn't feel like she was on the same level. She would take things one day at a time.

Her phone buzzed, pulling her out of her musing. Iris laughed out loud when she saw Melissa's picture appear on the display. She pressed the button on her steering wheel to answer the call with laughter still in her voice.

"You must have a spy camera on me or something because your timing is too perfect."

"Girl, quit playing. We don't need all of these preliminaries. Tell me about the date," Melissa said.

"Honey, I hope you're sitting down, because this is gonna be juicy."

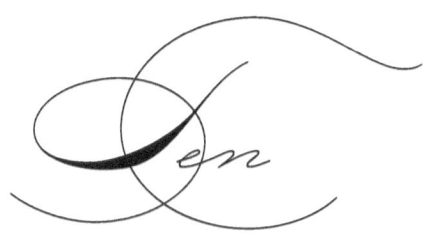

"Something is going on with my mother," Christian said to Shelby as he paced back and forth in their bedroom.

"Babe, calm down. I'm sure she's fine, come back to bed."

"I know you're unbothered because it's not your mother. It's not like you care for my mother anyway," he said, giving Shelby the full brunt of his frustration.

"Wait a minute." Shelby pushed the covers back and jumped out of the bed. "That's not fair, and I will not today or any day be your punching bag. You need to calm down."

"Admit it, Shelby, you don't like my mother. It's no secret."

"I don't have a problem with your mother, Christian. Yes, we got off to a rocky start but she hasn't said or done anything to me lately. I believe we squashed all of that at the clothing drive. I'm just saying, your mother is a grown woman, she's capable of taking care of herself. I'm sure she's fine. If she wasn't, you would have heard otherwise by now."

"There has never been a time in my life that I haven't heard from my mother in over a week. If you don't think something is wrong with that, then there is something wrong with you."

"You know what, I'm going to go downstairs before I say something to you that I can't take back. If you're that concerned then maybe you should call her, or better yet, go over to her house. I'm sure when you get there you'll see you've been overreacting. You're living your life and perhaps your mother is doing the same. Ha, maybe she has a man." Shelby stormed out of the bedroom, leaving the thought of Iris being booed up in Christian's mind.

She walked downstairs into the office and turned on the computer. She didn't have time to deal with Christian and his foolishness this early in the morning. She looked at the clock and saw it was 7:00am which meant it was nine o'clock at home. It was a good time for her to check on her own mother and to also check in with Kim.

Shelby tapped her manicured fingers on the desk while she waited for her mother to answer the phone.

"Hey, baby girl," Linda belted through the phone after a couple of rings.

"Hey, Mama. How are you doing?" Shelby asked, matching her mother's excitement.

"I'm doing good. How is California treating you?"

"Things are good. I start school next week so I've been trying to go out more to get used to the traffic. I wish I could have made it back there to get a few more of my things before school started, but it doesn't look like I'll have time to do it now. Everything has been happening so fast.

"Are you sure you don't want us to try to bring your car to you. I know you miss having your own vehicle."

"Mama, I gave you that car. You've been needing one for quite some time. Besides, you're going to ruin my surprise."

"What surprise? Are you pregnant?" Linda asked with anticipation.

"No, Mama. I'm not pregnant."

"Christian bought me a car. It's a convertible Audi. It's

gorgeous too. I'll have to send you some pictures.

"That's wonderful, Shelby," Linda replied. Shelby could hear the smile in her voice. "I'm so happy for you. That man really loves you."

Shelby wanted to shoot that statement down, especially after the fight she and Christian just had, but she chose not to. Her mother was right. He really did love her. She chose to change the subject instead.

"How is Sheena doing? She doesn't have that loser staying at my house with her does she? And I hope she's not getting too comfortable because as soon as I get back there I'm putting it on the market. The only reason I agreed to let her stay there is so that the house wouldn't deteriorate from being empty."

"Honey, Sheena is doing good. Wendell ain't nowhere in the picture. She's got herself a new man."

"What?" Shelby balked in obvious shock.

"Yes, honey. She be coming over here dressed all up, and she's driving around in a new car too. Well, it's a new used car because seeing as though she didn't have anything before, I think it's a pretty big deal."

Shelby couldn't believe what she was hearing. Her first thought was that Sheena was involved with some drug dealer. Classy, her sister was not so she couldn't imagine her being with someone that was legit. "Who is this man, Mama?"

"I don't know, she hasn't brought him by. I do know he's pretty wealthy and I believe his family is too. Just based on the stuff Sheena has told me."

"It's probably a drug dealer knowing her," Shelby said, no longer hiding her thoughts.

Linda's irritation with Shelby could be heard immediately

in her tone. One thing she didn't tolerate was her girls putting each other down. "Why does it have to be a drug dealer, Shelby? Didn't you get enough of people judging you when you were here? Why do you think a wealthy man could fall in love with you and the same not happen for your sister? I raised both of you girls the same. You have the same values and morals so don't do that to her. Speak what you know, not what you think. I will not have you cutting one another down."

Shelby felt like her mother had snatched a limb off a tree, cleared the leaves, and given her an old fashioned whooping with a switch. "I'm sorry, Mama, you're right. I hope she's found someone that is going to treat her right. Sheena is a beautiful girl. She hasn't always allowed men in her life that value her, so maybe being in my house and seeing what life can be like has given her a different perspective."

"Why do you always have to bring stuff back to you, Shelby? This man your sister is involved with has nothing to do with you." Linda was obviously irritated. "What else is going on? How's my son-in-law?"

"Shelby took the hint and fell in line with the change of subject. " He's doing good. Working hard as usual, but still doing good. He's freaking out a little because he hasn't heard from his mother."

"Is she okay?" Linda asked with concern.

"I'm sure she's fine, Mama. He didn't like it when I said she probably has a man." Shelby chuckled. "Lord knows I've been praying for it."

"Shelby, you shouldn't take things so lightly. His concerns may be justified."

"Trust me, Mama. If anything, and I do mean anything, was wrong with Iris, he would have been the first to hear.

She don't play that."

"Well, you just be sure to let me know how things turn out. In the meantime, I'll be keeping y'all in my prayers." Linda's voice trailed off a bit. "Shelby."

"Yes, Mama."

"I miss you. I hope I get to see you soon. It's weird having you so far away, but you girls have to live your lives. Hopefully we'll get to see each other soon."

"Yes, ma'am, we will. I promise. Besides, you have to come out here and see how I'm living. I can't wait to show you everything." Shelby talked a bit more about her life in California and listened to her mother catch her up on news about her other two sisters before ending the call.

"Shelby," Christian called from the door of the office, drawing her attention. Shelby raised her head, acknowledging his presence. "I'm going to swing by my mother's house before I head in to work. I'll give you a call later, okay?"

"Okay." Shelby pushed the chair back and walked around the desk. She didn't want them to part ways in anger, especially over something so senseless. She approached him and wrapped her arms around his neck, pulling him into a deep kiss. "I love you, Christian."

"I love you too," he replied, grabbing her butt and squeezing it. "I'll call you later."

Shelby bounced back to the desk. She couldn't stay mad at him if she tried. She grabbed her phone and headed to the living room. Her next call was to Kim. She was going to find out who this man was that Sheena was involved with if it was the last thing she did.

Eleven

"Mom, are you in there?" Christian yelled, while simultaneously banging on the door.

Iris snatched open the door. "Why are you knocking on my door like you're the police or something?" Iris stepped aside and allowed Christian to enter. She turned and walked away, leaving him to close the door.

Christian pressed the door closed and turned the lock before following his mother into the kitchen. Iris moved through the kitchen, unfazed by Christian's irritation. "Mom, I've been calling you. What's up with you not taking my calls?"

Iris poured herself a cup of coffee and turned to face her son. "I don't have to report my actions to you or anyone else. You clearly didn't inform me of your actions or decisions," she replied, glancing down at the wedding band on his finger.

"Don't deflect mother. I know this is your way of not answering my question. What have you been up to that keeps you so busy that you can't answer a call?"

"Honey, I am living my life like it's golden," Iris stated while spinning around with her hands in the air.

"What is that supposed to mean?" he asked, eyeing her suspiciously. "Shelby seems to think you have a man in your life."

Iris looked over her shoulder at her son. "I guess she's not as dumb as I thought she was. Kudos to Shelby."

"Wait a minute. That's my wife you're talking about, Mom."

"Exactly. You have your little wife that apparently you are willing to defend at all costs." She pulled on his shirt and lifted him from the stool he was sitting on. "So why don't you go home and focus on what's going on at your address and stop being so consumed with what I'm doing. You have your hands full enough."

"Are you seriously putting me out?"

"Yes, I am. Now gone, son. I have stuff to do and you're holding me up."

Christian stood on the other side of his mother's door in disbelief. She hadn't escorted him out of her house since he was a teenager going through his rebellious stage. What on earth was going on? He couldn't believe she was behaving this way. He also couldn't deny the pure joy that was written all over her face. Even when she offered a snide remark about Shelby, her tone was different and she had never stopped smiling the entire time he was with her. Maybe Shelby was right. Maybe there was a man in his mother's life. But who?

Iris watched her buzzing phone dance across the kitchen counter. She knew it could only be her annoying best friend, especially since her son had just left. Glancing at the clock on the wall, she realized she was running late for her appointment. Melissa had booked them for a mini spa day. She picked up her phone and pressed the accept button.

"I'm on my way. Christian stopped by, making me lose

track of time. I'll see you in a few minutes."

She arrived at the spa and dashed inside. Melissa stood, watching her with her arms folded, shaking her head. "Girl, you know good and well Evelyn is strict about her appointments. I had to come up with all kinds of excuses for your tardiness."

"Evelyn needs to calm down, especially with these prices, and I always tip her well. I'm sure she doesn't want to miss out on this money."

If Evelyn was upset, she didn't show it. She approached the ladies with a silver platter that contained two glasses of mimosa. "Are you ladies ready to be pampered?" she asked with a genuine smile. "I show that you're each getting a full body massage, manicure, pedicure, and hair styling."

"Yes, that's correct. I'm looking forward to the massage. I need to get these kinks worked out," Iris said.

"I'll bet you do," Melissa teased with an upturned lip.

Iris cut her a warning look, urging her to keep quiet. Melissa shrugged, disregarding Iris' threat.

"Right this way, ladies," Evelyn said, ushering them to the back." Melissa looped her arm around Iris' and took a sip from her mimosa.

"Let's do this."

The friends changed into plush white robes provided by the spa and proceeded to their individual massage rooms. Following the massage, they were escorted into the steam room.

"Ooh, girl, I needed that massage. I had to get those kinks out," Melissa said.

"Me too," Iris replied, wiping the sweat that was forming on her brow.

"So tell me, how are things going with you and Vincent?"

"Vincent is amazing. I keep telling myself to slow down, but he is such a sweetheart."

"I know the two of you have been inseparable. I won't lie, when you first started cancelling our weekly walks I felt some type of way. Dean, on the other hand, was constantly in my ear, reminding me of how we were when he and I first got together and how you were willing to give us our space."

"Exactly. Vincent and I are getting to know each other so we need that extra time." Iris dabbed more sweat. "I cannot get enough of this man. Every time we're together I feel closer to him, which is so weird." Dropping her head, Iris continued. "As much as I enjoy him, I must admit, I don't like feeling vulnerable."

Melissa moved closer to her friend. "Iris, if you're always guarded and never willing to be vulnerable you won't ever reap the benefits of everything you're meant to have. You can't be afraid of things going wrong or failing. A failure is a setup for success. You know this. We're not teenagers. Think about it. The failures of your past relationships taught you what you are willing to accept now."

"I want this to work, Melissa. Vincent is like no man I've ever come in contact with. He's handsome, sophisticated, clearly educated, and he really seems to like me."

"Ooh, Iris."

"What!" Iris balked.

Melissa pointed her finger at Iris' nose and started twirling it. "Somebody's been chimney sweeping."

Iris pulled her head back, preventing Melissa from touching her nose. "I don't know what you're talking about."

"Oh, yes you do. Don't even try it. I know you too well. Now spill it."

"There is nothing to spill. Isn't it about time for us to get

out of here. I'm about to burn up."

"I'll just bet you are with your little nasty self. Don't be trying to run now. You are busted."

The timer sounded, freeing Iris from Melissa's inquisition. "I guess you'll never know," Iris teased as she rose to exit the sauna.

Melissa was on her heels. "You want to bet."

Twelve

"Tell me something. Why do we keep staying at these hotels? My house is much better than any of these rooms we frequent. You're my woman and I'm your man. I have nothing to hide and I believe you when you say that you don't either. But, I'd be lying if I continued to pretend some things don't bother me. You never let me pick you up from your house. As a matter of fact, I don't even know where you live."

Iris rose from Vincent's arms and climbed out of bed. She reached for a robe to cover her nakedness but decided against it. She turned to face him so that he could get the full view. "Nobody is enjoying all of this, but you." She placed her hands on her hips and turned from side to side. She watched as his lips curved up into a smile. "I'm not ready to spend the night at your home with the staff and all of that.

Vincent eased from under the sheets and stood next to her, pulling her body closer to his. He kissed her on the forehead. "But, you won't even let me pick you up when I take you out. We always have to meet. What's up with that?"

"Because, Vincent, I told you…" her words trailed off as Vincent kissed her on her neck and then her lips. He drew her closer until there was no space between them. There was no more need for conversation as she surrendered to his touch.

Following their tryst, Iris showered and got dressed. While applying her makeup, Vincent approached her from behind and wrapped his arms around her. He kissed her on her ear and turned her to face him.

"You know I care about you, right?" he asked.

"Of course I do. I care about you too."

"I'm ready to take our relationship to the next level. I know you love your privacy, but I want to show you off. It's time for us to go public."

Iris let out an audible sigh. She treasured her life as a private citizen and she didn't want that to change. She and Vincent had done a good job of keeping their relationship away from the cameras and the prodding public. She hadn't even shared the extent of their relationship with her son.

"Listen," Vincent said, lifting her chin so that she was looking him in the eye. "I promise to protect you. I'll never let anyone harm you or make you uncomfortable. You never even have to speak a word. I want you by my side and nothing is going to change that."

"Those are some strong words you're speaking, Vincent. I don't know what all of this even means."

"There's a movie premier tomorrow night. I want you to go with me. Walking the red carpet, by my side as my lady." He took her by the hand and sat her down in a nearby chair. "I'm not sure what you heard about me before we got involved, if anything. Iris, I'm not a womanizer, never have been. I also don't jump in and out of relationships or beds. I've been looking for the right woman for a long time. Most women view what I have and my outward appearance and they desire me for vain reasons. You never did that. I believe when you look at me, you see *me*. Not stuff. That's the woman I want by my side."

Iris found it hard to resist Vincent's plea. She cared a great deal for him, and even found herself falling in love with him. However, she still didn't know exactly where their relationship was going, if anywhere. A public relationship equaled a very public breakup if it ever came to that. What if he was the one? Self-preservation could cause her to lose the best man that had ever entered her life. She closed her eyes and took a deep breath.

"I'll do it," she said, barely above a whisper.

"What was that?" Vincent probed placing his hand up to his ear in an exaggerated motion.

"I said, I'll do it," Iris said much louder than either of them anticipated.

"Well, alright." Vincent lifted her from the chair, pulling her into a warm embrace. He gave her a peck on the lips and turned her around. "Go finish getting ready, sweetheart. I'm hungry."

Iris returned to the vanity and applied lipstick, the only application she had not yet completed when Vincent interrupted her. Up until this point, Christian didn't know of her relationship with Vincent. Although he was the building contractor for Vincent's studio expansion, they hadn't discussed it. Iris' initial thought was that she should notify her son before the news hit tabloid TV. With a sinister grin she looked into the mirror. Maybe he should get a big shock the same as she did when he announced his marriage.

~~❧~~

The night of the premier provided all of the glitz and glamour Hollywood was known for. The limo pulled up to the Chinese Theater. The attendant opened the door and

Vincent stepped out. He reached for Iris' hand and helped her out of the car. She smoothed her pleated orange halter gown and steadied herself on beige mesh and silver glitter, crystal embellished pumps before stepping away from the car and falling in stride with Vincent.

The flash from the cameras was blinding. Iris resisted the urge to shield her eyes with her hand. She held Vincent's hand tightly as they moved forward on the red carpet. She plastered on a camera ready smile and made every effort to represent him. She took long strides, hoping the red carpet experience would end as quickly as possible.

"Ooh, is that your mom?" Shelby belted out, hitting Christian on the arm.

"What are you talking about?" Christian asked, rubbing his arm where Shelby hit him.

Pointing at the television, she yelled with excitement. "There, on the red carpet." Shelby picked up the remote and pressed the rewind button. "See, there she is. I thought that was her."

Christian sat up on the couch and squinted his eyes. His forehead wrinkled, pulling his eyebrows closer together.

"Oh, my God. Is she with Vincent Garret?" Shelby asked in disbelief. "I knew they were eyeing each other at that party but that was over a month ago. Maybe that's why you haven't heard much from her lately. Your mama is getting her swerve on." Shelby jumped up from the couch and twisted her hips.

"Shelby, sit down. Don't disrespect my mother."

"Christian, don't start. You know I'm kidding around." Dropping the remote back on the couch, Shelby turned back to her husband and said, "I'm only messing with you. I'm happy for your mom. She certainly looks happy. I'm going

to the kitchen. You want something?"

"No, I'm good." Christian never took his eyes off the screen.

"Suit yourself, I'll be right back."

Christian pulled out his phone and dialed his mother's phone number. He wasn't completely surprised when she didn't answer. The show they were watching was a live show. The premier was for the biggest movie of the year, and Shelby enjoyed watching the entertainment shows. Looking down, Christian's hands curved into a fist. He was going to find out what was going on between his mother and Vincent Garrett before the night was over.

Iris felt her phone buzzing in her small clutch. Once the red carpet walk was finished, she eased her phone out and viewed the display. She chuckled inwardly when she saw she had a missed call from Christian. There was no doubt that he had seen the footage of her and Vincent on the red carpet. *Suits him right,* she thought. Her son could dish it, but apparently he couldn't take it. Iris snuggled closer to Vincent as they headed into the theater to take their seats.

The movie was fantastic. Iris was happy she relented and decided to go with Vincent. She received a few stares from onlookers but nothing she didn't feel she couldn't handle. Following the movie, there was a reception where Vincent introduced her to the director, executive producers, and a few of the lead and supporting actors.

"I could get used to this," she whispered in Vincent's ear, bringing an instant smile to his lips.

"See, sweetheart, I told you it's not that bad. You keep

being beautiful both inside and out and there's no limit to what I will do for you. Starting with taking you home with me tonight."

Iris opened her mouth to protest, but words were unable to escape before Vincent covered her lips with his.

The night was long and by the time all of the events were over, Iris was desperate for a bed, any bed. They arrived at his mansion and were immediately greeted by a few members of Vincent's staff.

"This isn't fair," Iris protested. "What on earth am I going to sleep in?"

Vincent raised an eyebrow and gave a half smile.

"Stop being mannish, Vincent. I'm serious."

"Relax, I got you. You can sleep in one of my pajama tops, or even a t-shirt. If none of that suits you, I can have a member of the staff go out and pick something up for you."

"That won't be necessary. I'll make due with a t-shirt."

Iris looked around at the breathtaking estate. She thought it was beautiful the last time she was there, but with the house being put back in order with the exquisite furnishings that belonged in the living room turned ballroom and the dining room turned dining hall, she was left speechless. She felt like a child that was visiting her rich uncle's house. Terrified at the thought of breaking anything, she kept her hands to herself.

Vincent noticed the shift in her demeanor. He grabbed her around her waist and pulled her closer to him. "Sweetheart, this is just stuff. Nice stuff of course, but still stuff. When I leave here, I can't take any of it with me. While I'm here, if something happens to any of it, it's insured and I'm blessed to have enough that I can replace it. Don't be intimidated by what you see. Make yourself at home. I wouldn't have

brought you here if I didn't want you here."

He walked her over to the couch, sat down, and pulled her feet up into his lap. He carefully removed her shoes and massaged her feet. He pressed his thumbs into the middle of her foot, causing her to moan in delight. "Oh, you like that, huh?" he asked as he skillfully continued to knead her feet.

Iris allowed her head to rest on the back of the couch while her man pampered her. She felt so comfortable with him, like she had known him forever. Her phone buzzed again, pulling her from the euphoric state she was in. She ignored the call. After a brief pause, her phone buzzed again.

Vincent peered at her and then at her clutch where her phone was located. "Are you going to get that?" he asked, becoming frustrated.

"It's probably Melissa wanting to know how things went tonight. I can call her tomorrow. Now, can we please get back to my foot rub. That felt amazing."

Vincent eyed her suspiciously, but honored her request. Once again, her phone started buzzing. "Whoever it is must really want to talk to you." He eased her feet off his lap. "Please take the call." He stood to leave the room but Iris reached up and eased him back down.

"This won't take long." She pulled her phone out of her purse and viewed the display. Three missed calls from none other than Christian. Her frustration mounted as she dialed back his number.

"So you are alive I see," Christian said sarcastically.

"Don't go there with me, son. What's going on? Why are you blowing my phone up? Is someone dead or something?"

"Mother, don't be so dramatic. If you weren't being so secretive lately I wouldn't have to blow up your phone. I've called you four times this evening. Were you that busy that you couldn't receive a phone call?"

Wait a minute. You are not that grown. I'm still your mother. To answer your question, yes, I was quite busy. For your information, I'm still quite busy, so since this doesn't appear to be a life threatening emergency, I will talk to you later." Iris pulled the phone away from her ear and was about to press the button to end the call when she heard Christian call out to her.

"Mom, don't hang up."

She pressed the phone to her ear once again. "What is it? I told you, I'm in the middle of something."

"What's going on between you and Vincent Garrett? You know I have a huge contract with him. Is he using that to take advantage of you?" Anger spewed from Christian's lips.

"What goes on in my personal life is not your concern. For your information, Vincent and I are quite fond of each other. I see as much of him as I can, and I will continue to do so. And so that we are clear, what he and I have going on has nothing to do with you, or your business. Now, as I said before, I will speak with you on tomorrow. Goodnight, son." Iris ended the call before Christian could protest any further. She pressed the power button so that she and Vincent would have an uninterrupted evening. She turned back to him and came closer. Laying in his arms, she placed her hand on his cheek and pulled his face to hers. "Now, where were we."

Iris and Vincent sat across from each other at the breakfast table. His personal chef placed a gorgeous array of foods before them. Iris reached in the basket and placed a freshly baked croissant on her plate. The sweet buttery topping made the treat appear more like dessert than breakfast. Next, she scooped out various melons and added them to the plate. Lastly, she placed perfectly cooked eggs and bacon in the empty space remaining on her dish."

Taking a bite of her croissant, she closed her eyes and savored the taste. When she opened her eyes, Vincent was looking at her, smiling.

"I take it you're enjoying your breakfast," he said without breaking eye contact.

"Yes, I am. This is delicious. I don't know how you are still in shape eating meals like this."

"I'm glad you're enjoying it. Now you see why I exercise so much." Vincent pushed his plate away. "How would you feel about us spending the day together here at the house. You've only been here once and that was for the dinner party. I want to show you around, you know give you the official tour."

"Have you forgotten I don't have any clothes," Iris replied, pulling on the robe she was wearing that belonged to him."

"No, I haven't forgotten. I've already taken care of that.

I had my fashion stylist to come by this morning while you were asleep. She looked at the gown you wore for the premier last night and agreed to put together a few things for you. She should be back at any moment with both clothes and shoes for you."

Iris opened her mouth to protest, but Vincent put his hand up, stopping her. "Finish your breakfast, sweetheart. There's no need to debate. It's already handled."

She liked the fact that Vincent was a take charge man, but still she was cautious. She was controlling enough herself. There was no way she would let a man be equally as controlling of her. He'd better be glad she was enjoying herself and the delicious meal otherwise there would have been a rebuttal. She stabbed a piece of cantaloupe with her fork and put it in her mouth. One sure way to keep her mouth closed was to fill it with food.

After breakfast, Iris decided to relax in the bedroom, alone, while Vincent tended to his affairs. She heard a knock on the door and stood to open it. She found him standing on the other side with an arm full of garments. He had a bag that contained a couple pairs of shoes. Inside the bag was a pair of running shoes and sandals. Iris stepped to the side, allowing him room to enter. She reached to relieve him of some of the items but he kept walking.

Vincent placed the clothes on the bed and laid the shoes next to them. He took the top off the shoe box and Iris noticed the box containing the running shoes also held a few pairs of socks. Tucked in the midst of the clothes was a small lingerie bag that contained panties and a couple sports bras.

Iris pulled out the undergarments and looked at Vincent while tilting her head. "She bought underwear too?"

"Of course, I figured she needed to grab all of the necessities since you didn't come prepared to sleep over. Although I'm glad you decided to stay last night."

Iris picked up the hangers containing the clothes and sifted through the selection. She opted for a pair of capris and a fitness tee. Another tap on the door captured her attention. Iris watched as one of the housekeepers brought in a small wrapped basket containing female toiletries. She placed the basket in the bathroom and swiftly exited the room.

"Really, Vincent? You happened to have wrapped baskets containing women's toiletries laying around? I take it you entertain a lot of female companions." Iris started toward the bathroom but was halted by Vincent's hand on her arm."

He turned her to face him. "I have never lied to you, Iris. I told you in the beginning I am not a womanizer. Before you allow yourself to get upset over nothing, let me explain because I have nothing to hide. It's no secret, I have a big house. I entertain out of town guests quite frequently. As a courtesy to my guests, my staff keeps these baskets on hand. We have them for both males and females. Next time when you come, you can bring your own clothes and toiletries and you won't have to feel like I have a hidden agenda."

"I'm sorry. I overreacted. Of course you would have something like this for your guests. If a hotel can do it, so can you," she replied, teasing. "I'm going to shower and get dressed. I'll be out in a little bit."

"Vincent leaned over and kissed her. I'll be in my office. Do you remember where it is?"

"Yes, it's in the east wing, right?"

"That's my girl. Meet me in there when you're done. We can take our tour of the grounds at that time."

Iris dashed into the bathroom and stood in the three hundred sixty degree shower. The shower was custom designed. Each wall, including the door, had flat panel shower heads built in. In addition, there was a rainfall shower head hanging overhead. She pressed the waterproof computerized panel and disabled the overhead spray. The last thing she needed was for her beau to have a hairdresser come waltzing in to do her hair.

Iris finished her shower and used the remaining pins from her evening hairstyle to pull her hair up off her neck. She dressed and headed downstairs to Vincent's office. As she approached the office, she overheard him speaking to someone on the phone regarding the construction project for the studio expansion. She hated to eavesdrop, but if that was her son on the phone she wanted to know what was going on. She also struggled to believe that Vincent's feelings for her were completely genuine. She hoped they were but couldn't be sure.

"Did you need something, ma'am?" a male staff member asked, startling her.

"Oh no," she said, stuttering. "Vincent asked me to meet him down here. He's on the phone so I didn't want to go inside and interrupt."

"Yes, ma'am," the man said, nodding his understanding." Iris wasn't convinced he believed her, but it was partly true.

The conversation between Iris and the staff member caught Vincent's attention. He turned his chair around and beckoned for Iris to enter the office. She took a seat on the burgundy leather sofa that sat to the right of his desk in front of a huge oak wall of bookshelves.

Vincent continued his conversation in the same manner in which he had started before he knew she was in the hall.

He completed conducting his business and ended the call. Rising from the desk, he walked over and pulled Iris to her feet.

"Are you ready to go, sweetheart?"

"I sure am," Iris answered, feeling guilty for eavesdropping.

Vincent took her by the hand and led her out of the office. They continued until they were outside the mansion in the back yard. He walked her over to a stylish, top of the line golf cart and helped her climb aboard. Once she was settled, he went around to the other side and slid on the seat underneath the steering wheel.

We have a lot of ground to cover so I think you'll feel more comfortable riding. We can get out and walk throughout the tour. Vincent took her to the tennis and basketball courts first. Each court had a supply closet outside the gate which housed the tennis rackets and balls for each sport. Next, he took her to the vegetable garden and orchard, followed by a tour of his small vineyard.

Throughout their trip they engaged in conversation about their upbringing, families, and future goals. Vincent pulled the cart over so that they could get out and walk for a little while. Iris chased butterflies in the flower garden, bringing laughter from Vincent. He walked her over to a pond that contained two beautiful white swans. A manmade waterfall was built on the side of the pond with enough land between the two to host a party. The lush green grass reminded Iris of the turf on a football field. Tears formed in her eyes. Vincent noticed the change in her and escorted her to a white marble bench nearby.

"What's wrong?" he asked, taking her hand in his.

"Nothing really. Your property is beautiful. When we started talking about family and then I saw this, it made me think about my son."

"Christian?"

"Yes, Christian. He's my only son, my only child, for that matter. I looked at this landscape and thought about how much I had looked forward to him getting married. The first woman he was engaged to left him at the altar. The church was beautiful and full of guests. When he suffered that devastating blow, I told him when he met the right woman, I would give him the biggest outdoor wedding. Being out here reminds me of the fact that I won't be able to keep that promise. My son got married in Tennessee to a woman I had never even heard of, and to add insult to injury, I wasn't there. I wasn't even invited. I didn't learn about his marriage until he was home with his new bride."

Vincent placed his arms around Iris to comfort her. He wanted to take away her pain, but he wasn't sure how he could.

"I wish things could have been different. I wish I was there. He didn't give me the opportunity to agree or disagree. He didn't allow me to be there for the biggest day of his life. The fact that her mother was there, hurts that much more. They gave her more consideration than they did me. Had my son told me of his decision I would have been on the first plane there. Like it or not, I would have smiled proudly, seeing my son become a husband."

Looking around at the grounds, Vincent was reminded of the relatives that he had allowed to have weddings in the very spot they were sitting in. Suddenly, he had an idea. Not sure how she would take it, he approached the subject gingerly.

"I can only imagine the hurt you must feel. We can't change the past. However, we can alter the future." He

turned her face to his and looked her in the eyes. "From what you've told me, Christian didn't have much of a wedding, they basically exchanged vows in front of a preacher. As the mother of the groom, since you couldn't be there for the wedding, what do you think about hosting a reception for them. You can have it right here and invite both his friends and family. We could have her family to fly in as well. I'll cover the reception related expenses. When it comes to weddings, the reception is usually the best part anyway. Everybody likes a party."

The tears Iris had been holding back spilled from her eyes. "You would do that for me?"

"Absolutely. You're my lady and I'll do whatever it takes to make you happy."

Iris got up from the bench and sat in Vincent's lap. She wrapped her arms around his neck and pressed her lips against his. "You are the most amazing man I have ever had the pleasure of being involved with." Her heart was full of love for Vincent. She wanted to declare her true feelings for him, but she couldn't risk it. Instead, she kissed him deeper.

Fourteen

Iris pressed the call button on her steering wheel and waited impatiently for Melissa to pick up.

"Well, look who's alive," Melissa said, in lieu of a greeting.

"Don't start with me, girl. Besides, I'm too excited, not even you can throw me off."

"Do tell," Melissa replied anxiously.

Iris maneuvered her car into the left lane and merged onto the 405. "Last night following the premier and the after parties associated with it, Vincent insisted I stay at his house. My plan was to pick up my car and head home but he wouldn't hear of it. His house is amazing, but that's another story entirely."

"Push pause," Melissa interjected. "You spent the night with him?"

"It's not like it's the first time. Anyway, like I was saying…"

Melissa made a screeching sound emulating a car putting on breaks. "How did you think you were gonna fast forward past all of those juicy details. I knew it. When we went to the spa and you were in there glowing and stuff. I knew that man had swept your chimney."

"Melissa, will you please focus. What I have to tell you is big." Iris was becoming irritated with her friend's constant interruptions.

"Okay, girl, tell your story, but please know I'm putting a pin in that overnight action. We'll get back to it."

Iris pressed more firmly on the gas pedal, accelerating her car to pass a slow moving vehicle. "This morning Vincent gave me a full tour of his property. When we got to the flower garden, I mentioned how I wanted to give Christian an outside wedding before he ran off and eloped in Tennessee. Long story short, he suggested I give Christian and Shelby a reception and invite our friends and family as well as hers. But that's not the best part."

"Is he paying for it?" Melissa asked.

Disregarding Melissa's last statement, Iris continued. "He offered to let us use *his* property for the reception. When I tell you it is more elaborate than any venue I could have selected in all of Los Angeles County, I am not exaggerating."

"Wow, you must have put it on that brother."

"Seriously, Melissa. Do you ever think of anything else?" Iris exited the freeway.

"Girl, it's not often that someone finds new love at our age. We have passed the half century mark. I'm enjoying this. What did you say?"

"I told him I would have to talk it over with Christian and Shelby first and if they are in agreement I would gladly accept his offer. I'm headed to their house now. Hopefully, they're home."

"Don't tell me you drove all the way over there without calling."

"I sure did." Iris pulled into their driveway and parked. "I'm here now. I'll call you back and let you know how it goes." She turned the car off and tossed the keys inside her purse.

"I'll be waiting to hear. Talk to you later."

"Okay, bye."

Iris tucked her purse under her right arm and stepped out of the vehicle. She approached the front door and rang the doorbell. When she didn't hear any movement, she rang the bell again followed by a knock using the newly installed ornate brass door knocker.

"Coming!" Shelby called out, causing an instant eye roll from Iris. Shelby pulled the door open and greeted her mother-in-law with a smile. "Hello, Ms. Tyler."

"Hi, Shelby, is Christian here?"

"Yes, he is. He's out by the pool." Shelby stepped aside and allowed Iris to enter.

"Good, I need to speak to the two of you."

"Okay." Shelby stepped quickly, escorting Iris through the kitchen out to the pool. She looked over her shoulder. "By the way, you were stunning last night. You were wearing that dress."

As much as she tried to resist, Iris' lips curved up into a smile. "Thank you."

Christian was busy swimming laps when his wife and mother walked up. He immediately exited the pool and accepted the towel Shelby handed him. He patted himself down with the towel, removing as much moisture as possible. Christian lifted his arms to embrace his mother, but Iris stepped back.

The three laughed at Iris' quick motion. "That's okay, son. You're pretty wet. I'd rather stay dry."

"What brings you by? Seeing as though you weren't the least bit interested in talking to me last night."

"I didn't come to fight. I came to talk to the both of you about something very important."

Christian wrapped the towel around his waist. "Okay, we

can talk over here." He walked over to the outdoor lounge area followed by Iris and Shelby. He waited until they were seated before taking a seat of his own.

Shelby offered to get them drinks to which Christian and Iris both declined.

"What's this about, Mother?" Christian asked, not bothering to beat around the bush.

Iris jumped right into her reason for being there. It was obvious to her that Christian was still upset about the night before. It was best that she got straight to the point. "We all know I was very upset about not being invited nor informed of your wedding until after the fact."

Christian threw his hands in the air, revealing his frustration with his mother's speech. Shelby shot him an angry look.

"Go on, Ms. Tyler," she said.

"Thank you, Shelby." Iris cleared her throat and raised her head a bit higher. "As I was saying, I always thought I would be there when my son got married. Since you're already married that's a wish that will not be fulfilled. At least not with this wife."

"What?" Shelby snapped.

Iris continued as if her last statement wasn't offensive. "I was talking to a dear friend of mine and that friend had a great idea."

"Would this friend happen to be Vincent Garrett?" Christian asked with a hint of irritation.

"Christian," Shelby called through clutched teeth.

"As a matter of fact, it *is* Vincent. Anyway, he and I were talking and he asked me what I thought about giving you a reception. We could invite our friends and family, and Shelby, you could have your friends and family to fly out

here for the event. What do you think?" Iris was hopeful.

Shelby jumped up from her seat. "I think that's a great idea. It'll take a great deal of planning, but I know we could pull it off." Without warning, Shelby wrapped her arms around Iris, pulling her into a tight hug. Shelby's reaction proved there was no need for further discussion. The decision had been made.

Finally freeing herself from Shelby's embrace, Iris smiled broadly. "I guess we have a reception to plan."

Fifteen

"Can you believe it?" Shelby danced circles around her husband. "Your mother is giving us a reception. And we can invite everyone. This is awesome. I guess she's finally accepting our marriage. I'm so happy. Oh my goodness, I have so much to do. I need to get a dress and come up with a color scheme. I have to call everyone. I don't know how I'm going to fit this in with school, but I'll figure it out. First, your mom asked me to help with the fashion show and now this. There *is* a God."

Shelby spoke until she was breathless. Christian was happy to see his wife so excited, but for some reason he couldn't put his finger on, his mother's offer seemed insincere. One thing he knew about his mother was that she didn't let things go easily. Her sudden change of heart had red flags plastered all over it. He didn't know what it was, but his mother was up to something.

"Sweetheart," Christian said to Shelby, taking her wrist and pulling her down next to him. He lovingly peered into her eyes. "I know you're excited and so am I. This is a big deal. Please take things slow. Like you said, you already have a lot going on, and a reception will involve an enormous amount of work. Don't overwhelm yourself with this, okay."

"Christian, what's going on? You don't seem the least bit excited. I always dreamed of having a big beautiful wedding and reception. I gave up that dream when you asked me to elope. I felt like marrying you was more important that the wedding. This reception will give me the opportunity to recapture a portion of that dream. Best of all, we'll be able to include our friends and family. Every time I call home I have to hear my sisters and my friends fuss about us not inviting them when we got married. This could be our redemption."

Shelby placed her hands on both sides of Christian's face and pecked him on the lips. "Don't you see, now your mother can be involved and perhaps she and I can have a fresh start."

Seeing the excitement in his wife's eyes, Christian dared not to voice his concerns. There was no way he could deny his wife the reception she deserved. He was so determined to marry Shelby that he didn't consider what she was sacrificing by eloping. Wrapping his arms around her waist, he pulled her in close. "Whatever it takes to make you happy, I'm willing to do. If a reception is what you want, a reception you shall have. I love you, Shelby."

"And I love you too, sweetheart." Shelby kissed her husband and jumped up from his lap. She pulled her phone from her pocket and selected her mother's phone number. "I've got to call my mama."

Iris pressed the unlock button on the key fob as she approached her vehicle. She was elated over Shelby's excitement, but she could've done without the attitude Christian was giving her. She didn't know what his problem was, but she wasn't in the mood to deal with it right now. There would be plenty of time for that. For now, she had a reception to plan. Her son's reception was going to be exactly what she wanted it to be. Nothing more and nothing less. There was no way she would allow Shelby to turn her son's reception into a hoedown.

Securing her seatbelt, Iris started her car and pulled out of the driveway. She had barely reached the street when her phone started ringing. "My goodness, do you have a tracking device on me or something? I just pulled out of Christian's driveway."

"I figured you would have been gone by now," Melissa retorted. "When I didn't hear back from you, I thought maybe you had forgotten to call me back. How did it go?"

"It looks like I'm going to be planning a wedding reception."

"Really? They accepted the offer," Melissa paused for a moment before continuing with added emphasis, "from you?"

"And what is that supposed to mean, from me? Of course from me."

"I'm pretty shocked they didn't take the idea and throw one of their own instead of accepting your offer. Iris, everybody knows you're not fond of Shelby. Unless being with Vincent has given you a change of heart. Sounds to me like somebody has accepted her daughter-in-law," Melissa teased.

"I've told you not to call her that. She is Christian's wife, that's it.

"How are you going to pull this off, seeing as though you can't stand the bride. If you're planning the reception you will have to spend a lot of time together. You'll have to find out what she likes and plan the reception around it."

"Let's get something straight, the only reason I am doing this reception is because Vincent suggested it and offered his property. This will also help a little with my friends in the social circles I'm affiliated with. They questioned me a lot when they found out my son was married and didn't have a wedding here. Me doing this reception does not mean I like her. I still believe she's a gold digger and it's only a matter of time before Christian finds out. I hope it's before she bleeds his bank accounts dry."

"Girl, you are bold. I hope this plan doesn't backfire. You're my friend and I'd hate to see you get hurt, but I also hate to see you plotting to hurt your son's wife."

"My son's wife, huh? I like that. It has a cool ring to it and it says exactly how I feel about her. I feel like I've heard that statement before."

"You sure have, we read a book a while back with that title. Anyway, I can't sit here talking to you all day. I have a few things I need to get done around this house. If you need help with the planning, give me a call."

Sixteen

Music blasted from the speakers, as the runway filled with machine created fog. Multicolored lights danced across the stage as the guest anxiously awaited the appearance of the models. A spotlight shined at the back of the stage and the curtain parted. One by one the models of all shapes, sizes, and nationalities graced the runway, each bringing their own unique element.

With the fierceness of professional models, both male and female models showed off the latest fashion trends. A select few wore original designs from students at the Fashion Institute where Shelby attended. Camera flashes from photographers and attendees' cell phones blended in with the stage lighting. Once the final model returned to the rear of the stage, all of the models walked back onto the stage followed by Iris, Shelby, and Winifred.

The crowd cheered with a thunderous applause. Winifred allowed the crowd to calm before she spoke. "Whew, what an amazing show," she exclaimed. The crowd ignited with another uproar of applause. "It's all because of these ladies right here," Winifred said, pointing at Iris and Shelby. "Many of you are familiar with Ms. Iris Tyler. She heads up our fashion show every year. This year she brought her daughter-in-law on board, Mrs. Shelby Tyler, and this show has reached a new level." The crowd continued to applaud. Winifred continued, "We don't have our final totals yet, but so far we have raised three times the amount from last year's fashion show. Give yourselves a hand, ladies, as we all applaud you."

Iris gave a polite smile while inwardly she fumed. She looked over at Shelby who was smiling brightly. If she had to guess, Iris would say she was showing all of her teeth. She wanted to scratch Shelby's eyes out. She had worked hard to build up that fashion show over the years and just because Shelby brought colorful lights, a fog machine, and a few designs from that little school she attended, Winifred was acting like everything was perfect in the world and that Shelby sat on the shoulders of God.

She found Melissa in the crowd and gave her the inconspicuous look they shared when they felt someone was being extra. Melissa responded with a slight nod. Christian approached the stage with a bouquet of roses for Shelby. Iris was in the middle of rolling her eyes when she saw Vincent approach the stage with a bouquet that was twice the size of the ones Christian brought. For the first time all night, Iris had a genuine smile.

The couples, along with Winifred, exited the stage. "That was an amazing show, ladies," Vincent said. "How about we go out for a celebratory dinner, my treat of course."

"No, thank you," Christian said immediately.

"Ignore him, Vincent," Iris said with a wave of the hand. "We will be delighted to join you.

Shelby tugged on Christian's arm until he agreed to join them for dinner. The four headed out to a nearby restaurant. Vincent's notoriety got them seated immediately. Iris excused herself for a bathroom break, followed by Shelby leaving Christian and Vincent alone at the table.

"What's going on with you and my mom?" Christian asked bluntly with a hint of irritation.

Vincent was taken aback by Christian's question. They had maintained a good working relationship so he was a bit confused by Christian's tone. "Your mother and I care a great deal for each other. We're taking things day by day, seeing where it goes."

"Don't you think you're a bit old to be seeing where things go?"

"Hold on, man," Vincent said, raising his hand. The bass in his voice intensified.

The ladies returned to the table and saw the men with intense stares at each other. "What's going on?" Iris asked, looking from one man to the other.

Vincent stood and pulled Iris' chair out for her, and kissed her on the cheek before they sat back down.

They placed their orders and talked while they waited. "How are the plans for the reception coming along?" Vincent asked.

"We haven't made many plans so far," Shelby answered.

Cutting her off, Iris interjected, "I thought it would be best if we waited until after the fashion show was over before we started on the reception. With Shelby being in school and everything, I didn't want to overwhelm her with too many details. It's a lot to juggle."

Shelby disregarded Iris' comment. They had worked together for a couple of months on the fashion show and things had gone well, in her opinion. There was no need to rock the boat. Turning her attention to Vincent, she spoke with excitement and anticipation. "I'm looking forward to planning the reception. My husband will tell you, it's all I talk about."

Christian remained quiet for most of the meal. Iris eyed him. It was unusual for him not to involve himself in the flow of conversation. "Son, are you feeling okay? You're awfully quiet tonight."

"I'm fine. I have a lot of work to do, so I pretty much need to get home."

Vincent raised his hand to signal the server. "It looks like we've all finished eating. It has been an eventful night. I appreciate you and your wife joining us this evening, Christian."

"No problem. Thank you for inviting us."

Once Vincent paid the check, they all stood to leave. Walking towards the door, Vincent placed his hand on Christian's shoulder. "Hey, man, will you hang back for a moment?"

Iris turned around when she saw the men stop. Vincent gave her a wink and nodded toward the restaurant door. She and Shelby proceeded outside.

Christian stood with his arms crossed. "What's up, man?"

"Look, Christian. I have nothing but good intentions for your mom and myself. I care for her a lot and I'm coming to you man to man to let you know there is no need for hostility. She and I have been involved for a few months now and I have no plans of going anywhere. I'm past that whole player stage. I'm a grown man. I don't have time for those childish games."

"You know what man, I can respect you for that. I don't want to see my mom get hurt so naturally my defenses are up, but she does seem to like you. I'll give you that. I'm not

trying to get into what you and my mother have going on. I'd rather focus on our business relationship and let you and my mom do your thing. Do her right and we won't have a problem."

Vincent extended his hand to Christian and he shook it.

Seventeen

Iris reached into her overnight bag and retrieved a bag of toiletries. She walked into the en suite and placed the bag on the counter. Vincent followed her into the bathroom and wrapped his arms around her from behind. Iris leaned her head back, relishing in his embrace.

"I don't know why you don't leave that stuff here. It's a shame for you to have to keep hauling it back and forth."

She looked at him through the mirror, making eye contact without breaking their embrace. "I can't do that. Your space is yours, I can't interfere with that. I don't want you to think I have any high expectations. What we have is good. I can't have you thinking I'm trying to trap you."

Iris fought hard to keep her insecurities under wraps. She wanted to have more with Vincent but she dared not ask. Things were going well with them and she didn't want to mess that up by moving too fast.

Releasing the embrace, Iris turned to face him. "It's not like you're leaving stuff at *my* house. In fact, you've never even spent the night at my house."

"Let's be clear sweetheart, you've never invited me to stay at your house," Vincent replied, staring into her eyes. "It took you forever to tell me where you live."

Iris didn't expect Vincent to leave the comforts of his

mansion to stay with her in Inglewood which is why she hadn't invited him to stay. She brought up the fact that he hadn't stayed at her house as leverage to justify her decision to not leave items at his home. She could tell she'd struck a sore spot with him and she wasn't in the mood to argue. She wrapped her arms around his neck and pulled him into a kiss. "And I'm okay with that. There's no need of you staying over at my house when I'm willing to spend time with you here."

Vincent led her back into the bedroom. He sat down on the bed and pulled her onto his lap. "I don't have a problem with where you live. I would never lead you to believe that I view you as less than I am because of my achievements. I'm with you because I want to be, not because I have a hidden agenda."

"I know that, Vincent. You and I both know I live in Inglewood by choice, not because I have too."

"Of course I know better than that," Vincent laughed. "As protective as your son is over you, there is no way you would be anywhere other than where you want to be."

"I know that's right," Iris agreed, joining him in laughter.

Vincent pulled her hair to the side and kissed her on the neck and again behind her ear. The passion between them was undeniable. The more they were together the closer they became.

"I'm hungry, how about you?" Vincent asked.

"I ate about an hour ago. I'm not very hungry right now. Maybe in a little while. But, if you want something, don't let me stop you. I'll get something to drink and enjoy your company. "

"Okay. Get ready and we can go."

Iris grabbed her purse, leaving her overnight bag lying

next to the bed and they made their way downstairs. Vincent walked over to one of his male staff members and instructed him to retrieve Iris' overnight bag and to put it in the trunk of his car. He pulled her into the kitchen and sifted through the offerings. He turned to her with a look of disappointment.

"What's wrong? Do you want me to fix you something?" Iris asked.

"No, I don't see what I want. What I'm in the mood for isn't in this fridge. For that matter, it's not in this house."

"What are you in the mood for?"

"I want Polynesian food, and I know the perfect restaurant to get authentic Polynesian cuisine."

"Are you talking about Kahuna in Beverly Hills?"

"No," he chuckled lightly. "This place is much better than that." Vincent took Iris by the hand and led her out to his car. He opened the door and allowed her to slide into the seat. He pulled on the seatbelt and strapped her in, being sure to brush past her bosom. He grabbed her thigh and planted a kiss on her lips before moving over to his side and getting behind the wheel.

Vincent drove virtually in silence until they reached a small airport. Iris looked around with a puzzled expression. "Vincent, what are we doing here? I thought we were headed to a restaurant."

"We are," he replied with a sinister grin. "My favorite restaurant just happens to be in Hawaii."

"Hawaii!" Iris yelled. "I can't go to Hawaii. I'm not prepared for Hawaii. I don't have clothes or anything."

"Calm down, my dear. Your bag is in the trunk. I had Simon to get your overnight bag and toiletries while you and I were in the kitchen. We're only staying overnight. If we decide to stay longer, we'll go shopping. I'm sure you'll be able to find something you like in Maui."

Vincent parked his vehicle next to a small white jet and opened the trunk. A man in a black suit approached them and took the bags out of the trunk. The flight crew stood outside to greet them. The pilot and co-pilot introduced themselves to Iris, followed by the flight attendant. The man that took their bags introduced himself before stepping aside so that Vincent could escort Iris onto the plane.

The nine passenger vessel was breathtaking. The ivory leather seats complimented the polished woodgrain interior beautifully. After strapping in, Vincent told her the flight would be close to six hours.

"Oh, I know. I've been to Honolulu before. This will, however, be my first time going to Hawaii with you, and my first time flying in a private jet."

He laced his fingers with hers, raised her hand to his lips, and kissed it. Once they were airborne, Vincent drifted off to sleep. Iris laid her head on his shoulder and focused on the movie that was playing on the big screen television located in the cabin of the plane.

The flight was smoother than Iris expected. Given the size of the plane, she thought there would be a lot of turbulence. They exited the plane and were greeted by a driver waiting to take them to the restaurant and inn.

"We're going to a place called Mama's Fish House," Vincent said. "Hear me when I tell you, they have the best food on the island."

The driver took the twenty minute scenic route from the airport to The Inn at Mama's, where Vincent had reserved a room adjacent to Mama's Fish House. He pulled around to the inn. Vincent and Iris went inside to check in. After checking in, they were escorted to their beachfront suite.

Iris thought her heart would explode. She couldn't believe Vincent would go through such lengths to surprise her and to treat her special. She toured the expansive space, stopping in the living room to enjoy the breathtaking view of the beach. Vincent pulled her into an embrace and whispered in her ear.

"We don't have to leave tomorrow if you don't want to. We can stay for as long as your heart desires."

"Oh, Vince," Iris purred, kissing him with a fiery passion.

"Don't you get nothing started. We have dinner reservations, but I don't mind cancelling them."

Iris backed up with a giggle. "Okay, okay I'll behave. We came here for the food right?"

"Right," Vincent replied, smoothing his pants.

"Give me a moment to freshen up and I'll be ready to go." Iris escaped to the restroom. Pulling out her phone, she texted Melissa. **Girl, you won't believe where I am.**

Where? Melissa texted back immediately.

Maui!!! Vincent flew us here in a private jet saying he was hungry for authentic Hawaiian food. I cannot believe this.

Girl, you better keep that man. I wish Dean would do some stuff like that. I'd be stuck to him like glue.

You're a mess, Iris replied.

I'm not playing!

Iris laughed at her friend. **I have to go, we're about to go eat. Not sure how long we're staying. ttyl.**

Have fun! Melissa texted back.

Iris pulled out her compact and blotted the shine from her nose with the powder. She touched up her lipstick and squirted droplets of perfume. Smoothing out her hair, she looked in the mirror and smiled. She could not believe this was her life. Vincent was a gift from God and she could no longer deny what her heart was feeling. She was in love and it felt amazing.

~~🐚~~

The open air restaurant décor was true Hawaiian style. Iris admired the scenery while they waited briefly for their table. The tropical plants, colors, and artwork were beautiful. Once they were seated, their server placed a menu in front of each of them and took their drink orders.

"I'll have the Maui Margarita," Iris said.

Vincent added, "You can bring me the Marinero Daiquiri."

The server nodded and stepped away from the table.

Iris scanned the menu, delighted by the offerings. "They actually have their own fishermen that go out and catch this fish fresh every day?"

"Yes. Now you see why I said this is the best restaurant. Wait until you taste it. The food is amazing."

The server returned with their drinks. She placed their beverages in front of them. "Are you all ready to order, or would you like a little more time to look over the menu?"

"We're ready," Vincent replied. He paused, allowing Iris to place her order first.

The Mama's Stuffed Mahi-mahi sounds good. I believe I'll have that."

The server nodded and turned to Vincent, "And for you, sir."

"I would like the Makeweli ranch tenderloin filet and Tristan Island lobster."

Iris danced in her seat to the island sounds as she sipped on her drink. Vincent smiled at her.

"I'm glad you're enjoying yourself. Seeing you happy makes everything I do for you worth it." He reached across the table and caressed her hand.

The server returned with their meals, interrupting the intimate moment. Iris took a look at her dish and gushed with excitement. The mahi-mahi was stuffed with lobster and baked in a macadamia nut crust. She pulled off a piece and closed her eyes when the fork entered her mouth. Savoring each bite, she ceased all conversation with her companion.

"So, do I need to get myself a separate room while you and your meal enjoy the evening together?" Vincent teased.

She swallowed her bite and burst into laughter while wiping her mouth. "Was I that bad?" Iris asked in a whisper.

"Oh yeah, I thought you were about to start moaning," he replied, joining her in laughter. "I told you this place was the best. It's worth the flight."

"I agree with you completely."

After dinner, they decided to take a tour of the grounds and a walk on the beach. The temperature was perfect. A breeze from the ocean blew through Iris's hair, massaging her scalp. The sunset filled the sky with orange and red hues. Iris faked a yawn.

"Are you tired?" Vincent asked.

"I'm ready to go to the room. Can we go now?" Her tone was sensual and filled with seduction.

Vincent looked into her eyes and raised an eyebrow. He placed his arm around her waist and turned in the direction of their suite.

Eighteen

"How are the reception plans going?" Linda asked.

Shelby hadn't spoken to her mother in weeks. School was taking up most of her time. When she wasn't in school she was busy playing wife and homemaker to Christian. "So far it's not going. I've been quite busy lately that I haven't had much time to focus on it. Ms. Tyler and I are supposed to get together later today to go over some of the details."

"Is that woman finally acting like she has some sense?"

Sighing, Shelby carefully chose her words. She knew Linda's opinion of Iris was based solely on the information she had given her. Shelby tried to find a way to ease the tension she initiated between her mom and mother-in-law. "She's doing great, Mom. We don't see much of her these days since she and Vincent got involved, but when we do, she's pleasant."

"How that woman with her nasty attitude ended up with a billionaire boyfriend is beyond me. But you know what, it seems like that's how it goes. The ones that deserve it least always seem to end up with the good stuff happening to them."

"Mama, we can't say that about her. Granted, she was very upset about Christian and I getting married without her knowledge, but up until then from what I hear, she's

117

always been a kind and generous woman."

"Yeah, right," Linda snapped.

"Put yourself in her position, Mama. It's four of us but imagine if I was your only child and you found out I got married without telling you. Better yet, what if I never told you and you just happened to see me with my husband and I said guess what, Mama, this is my husband. How would you feel?"

"I don't know. I can't imagine."

"Well, that's exactly what happened with Ms. Tyler and us. She knew Christian was due home that day and when she came over to visit him, she saw me." Hearing her own words made Shelby's heart sink. She never gave serious thought to what that moment must have been like for Iris. Until now.

"Now, Shelby, you know when you girls are right, I'll stand with you. When you're wrong, I'll be the first to tell you. You and Christian were dead wrong with how you handled things. However, you're my daughter, and I still believe she was too hard on you. Especially with the way she embarrassed you at that mall when you first got there."

Shelby considered her mother's words as she sat on the couch. She could have held on to the ill feelings she had for Iris in the beginning but she felt like they served no purpose. Iris was making amends by giving them the reception. She and Christian were happy and enjoying married life. In her mind there was nothing left to do but move on.

She looked out the window and noticed Iris' car pulling up. "Mom, she just arrived. I'll have to let you go."

"Okay. I need to get in here and fix some pies anyway. Call me later and let me know how things went. If there's anything I can do to help, you know that I'm willing."

"I will, Mama, and I know you are. I love you."

"I love you too. Give Christian a kiss for me."

Shelby ended the call with her mother and walked to the front door. She pulled it open before Iris had a chance to ring the doorbell.

Iris eyed her. "Hello, Shelby."

"Hi, Ms. Tyler. Come on in. Can I get you something to drink? Water, juice, a glass of wine perhaps?"

"No, I'm fine for now. Maybe later."

"I have everything in the dining room. I figured we could work in there." Shelby escorted Iris into the dining room. She had bridal magazines, catalogs, and invitation samples laid out on the table.

"What's all this?" Iris asked.

"This is some of the stuff I've collected. I've seen some great ideas for the reception." She picked up the invitation samples. "These are a few of the invitation styles I like. I wanted to get your opinion on them. I'm open for suggestions." Shelby beamed. She couldn't believe she and Iris were sitting across from each other discussing her and Christian's reception. It had been months since Iris made the offer. Shelby almost said forget it, and plan one of her own due to the constant delays from Iris, but she didn't want a repeat of their wedding.

Iris sifted through the items Shelby had on the table. The more she examined the items, the more disgusted she became. She watched as Shelby flipped through the magazines, pointing out gowns and reception décor. She pulled out swatches of various colors, fabrics, and patterns. Shelby bounced around the room like a gushing bride.

Shaking her head, Iris took a deep breath and let it out slowly. "No, no, no. This simply won't do. You're thinking much too small, Shelby. These things may work where you're from, but they are not befitting for a Hollywood reception. Think about the venue. Vincent's home is exquisite." She held up the invitations. "Do these look exquisite to you?"

Shelby swallowed hard. She didn't appreciate Iris turning her nose up at her ideas. Basically, she had called her small minded in a subtle way. On top of that, she had insulted Shelby's hometown. Not wanting to start the day on a bad note, Shelby decided to hear her out. "What do you have in mind, Ms. Tyler?" She kept her tone even.

"First of all, you need to know these books are useless. You don't need to trouble yourself with all of the minor details. That's what an event planner is for. Although you're only having a reception, I have contacted Kareena Prajar. She's the best in the business. We have an appointment with her at one o'clock. When we conclude our meeting with her, I have scheduled a meeting at Francisco's on Rodeo Drive. I took the liberty of selecting a few gowns for you to choose from. If you don't find what you want from those, Francisco will custom design one for you. Your gown must be couture, not something off the rack or out of a magazine. I may not have had any input when you and my son were married, but I will make sure the reception is befitting."

Shelby was no longer upset. She never imagined the reception would be this elaborate. She decided to step back and let Iris take the lead. "This is great, thank you Ms. Tyler. Let me grab my purse and I'll be ready to go. Did you want to ride together or should I drive?"

Once again, Iris turned her nose up at Shelby. There was no way she was going to let Shelby embarrass her by going anywhere dressed like a gas station employee. Her ripped jeans and screen printed t-shirt were deplorable. "You're not wearing that are you?"

"I guess not. Give me a moment to change. I'll be down in a few minutes. Please make yourself comfortable." Shelby dashed up the stairs to find an outfit befitting her mother-in-law.

Nineteen

The ladies arrived at Kareena's office. Iris felt it was best that they drove separate vehicles. She told Shelby it was because she had other errands to run immediately following the meetings, but the truth was she didn't feel like being cooped up with Shelby all day.

They were greeted by the receptionist who notified Kareena of their arrival. Before they had the opportunity to take a seat, Kareena came out to get them. "It's so nice to see you again, Ms. Tyler." Turning to Shelby she continued, "You must be Shelby, our bride." Kareena offered both ladies a warm smile and handshake. "If you'll follow me, we can get started."

Shelby walked down the long hall, admiring poster sized photos of weddings and events Kareena had done. She brought them to a large room with several glass tables and modern art deco décor. Each table held a different color theme. Shelby walked over to the table that had a setting with gray, aqua, and navy options. She stepped away from that table and clapped her hands in delight at the black, white, and silver arrangement.

"Ooh, I really like this one," Shelby said when she saw the table with the fall colors of burgundy, orange, and yellow.

Iris rolled her eyes. She stood next to the table with the display of the arrangement she had previously picked out.

123

Being careful not to reveal her ill feelings towards Shelby to Kareena, she spoke as politely as she could muster. "Shelby, dear, will you please join us over here?"

"Sure," Shelby said, gliding over to where the ladies were standing.

Pointing to the table, Iris spoke with authority. "This is the arrangement and color scheme I have picked out."

Shelby looked down at the table and gave a modest smile. It wouldn't have been her first nor second choice, but she didn't want to make a scene. She rubbed her hands against the shimmery dusty rose fabric. She had to admit the gold and ivory accents really brought the design together. The plate settings were ivory with gold foil edging. Ivory and dusty rose napkins were held together with etched gold rings.

"Each invitation will be hand painted and designed by our master penmen." Kareena said as she handed Shelby and Iris samples of the invitations.

"These are very elegant," Shelby admitted, admiring the invitation.

"Thank you," Kareena said. "I will need your full guest list along with their addresses so that we can get these completed and mailed out in a timely manner." She pulled out another card marked Menu. "Here is the menu selected by Ms. Tyler. I hope you will find it to your liking."

Shelby scanned the menu. The entrees included grilled sirloin with béarnaise, roasted garlic potatoes and grapefruit scented asparagus, grilled pacific fish with piperade and rose lentils, and butternut squash ravioli with brown butter and crispy sage. She tried but failed to mask her frown. "Although this menu is quite impressive, I've never even heard of some of this stuff."

Iris expelled a sardonic giggle. "Don't be silly, dear. This menu is perfect. We're not having a fried chicken and barbeque rib type of event. The menu is appropriate for the occasion. Don't you agree?"

Stunned, Shelby pressed her lips together in more of a snarl than a smile. "I suppose you're right, not that I would have selected chicken and ribs anyway."

"Lastly, here is the cake," Kareena said, handing Shelby a picture of a beautiful five tier cake.

Shelby looked at the photo and immediately handed it back to Kareena. "That is a beautiful cake, however I would like something different. My mother-in-law has done such a wonderful job of picking out everything else for *my* reception that I must insist on taking this particular task off her hands. My husband and I will pick out our own cake."

"As you wish, Mrs. Tyler," Kareena replied, nodding.

Iris bore into Shelby with a penetrating glare. "Remember, dear, time is of the essence. I'm sure Kareena's calendar is very full. Who knows when you'll be able to get back in here to see her. We need to go ahead and finalize everything."

"It's not a problem." Shelby reached into her purse and pulled out a card with the name of a bakery along with the size and flavor of the cake she wanted. She handed the card over to Kareena, bypassing Iris. "When you suggested we have a reception here in L.A., Christian and I spent a day filled with cake tastings."

"Oh, I see." Kareena examined the card. "Ji-reh Bakery is actually one of the companies I work with. Their cakes are delicious and they always do an amazing job with the designs." She tucked the card away in a folder marked 'Tyler Reception' along with the other items related to the event. "Do either of you have any questions, suggestions, or anything before we conclude our meeting?"

"No," Iris spoke immediately, hindering Shelby from speaking. "Everything is in order. I know you will do an amazing job. We're off to Francisco's next."

"Splendid. I will be in contact. In the meantime, if you need anything don't hesitate to reach out." Kareena led the ladies out to the lobby and offered them each a parting handshake.

Iris walked ahead of Shelby, leaving no room for conversation. She called out to her, "Francisco is waiting for us, we must hurry." She jumped in her car and waited for Shelby to get into her vehicle before backing out.

The drive to Francisco's from Kareena's office was brief. Shelby considered calling Christian to inform him of how she felt things had gone at the event planner's office, but decided against it. She would have plenty of time to fill him in with the details when he got home from work. Iris was proving to be a piece of work and Shelby didn't like it one bit. Who did she think she was anyway. Shelby was tempted to call the whole thing off, but she quickly reconsidered. She mulled over the details in her mind of all that Kareena had presented to her. She did have good ideas, and as much as she hated to admit it, Iris' selections were stellar. Perhaps she was just being overly sensitive.

They arrived outside of Francisco's boutique and parked their cars. Shelby was determined to keep an open mind and to receive the assistance that Iris was so generously offering. The good thing was she and Christian were already married so Iris couldn't interfere with that. Could she?

~~👁~~

"Iris, how are you, my dear?" an Italian man with jet black hair approached Iris with arms outstretched. He gave her a quick embrace and kissed her on each cheek.

"Francisco, darling. How are you?"

"I'm well." Noticing Shelby standing nearby, Francisco turned to her and said, "Hello, gorgeous. Are you our bride?"

"Yes, I am," Shelby said, extending her hand.

Disregarding her hand, Francisco pulled her into a hug. "Welcome, welcome." He took both ladies by the hand and escorted them to a sitting area located at the center of the boutique.

Shelby looked around at the dresses displayed throughout the space. They ranged from mini dresses to floor length gowns in a variety of colors and textures. She noticed there was only one of each. Francisco's assistant approached them with a silver tray carrying two glasses of champagne.

"I have the gowns you selected in the back, Ms. Tyler." Francisco signaled to his assistant to bring out the gowns. He reached out to Shelby and helped her to her feet. He pulled a tape measure from his pocket. Delicately taking her measurements, he recorded the numbers in his iPad.

The assistant rolled out a rack with several gowns. The gowns were ivory, champagne, blush, and pewter in color. Some of the gowns were lace, silk, and taffeta while others were satin. Iris and Shelby both approached the rack and looked through the offerings. As a fashion stylist, Shelby was enamored with the gowns. She pulled several from the rack and held each one up in front of her.

"Are you ready to try some on?" Francisco asked.

"Yes, I am."

The assistant retrieved the gowns Shelby selected and placed them in a spacious room. She stayed in the room to help her put the gowns on. One by one, Shelby tried the gowns on and walked out to show Iris.

Iris gave her opinion of each gown. For the gowns that she didn't like, she immediately dismissed Shelby with the flick of her hand. Gowns she wasn't sure about received a hunched shoulder response. When Shelby stepped out in a gown that pleased Iris, she was rewarded with a nod and smile.

Two hours later, Shelby was exhausted. She decided on a gown that both she and Iris were pleased with. Iris gave her a hug, patting her on the back in the process.

"Shelby, dear, you can go now. I need to talk to Francisco about my dress. Give my son a hug for me."

Melissa sat across from Iris, staring at her best friend in disbelief. "Girl, you didn't."

"I sure did, she thought she was running things, I let her know real fast that I was the one in control of this reception."

Taking a sip from her cup of coffee, Melissa placed her elbow on the table and allowed her head to rest in her hand. "So, let me get this straight, you didn't let her make any of the decisions?"

"She got to pick the cake. Girl, she had the nerve to try to get all big and bold talking about 'my husband and I will pick our own cake.' Apparently they had already gone cake tasting and picked out one they liked. The only reason I didn't object to the cake was because Kareena said the bakery they selected was one that she also deals with.

"Honey child, let me tell you, you are a bold one. I can't believe Christian didn't have any feedback because you know she told him when she got home."

"I wish he would say something to me." Iris raised her glass and drank some water. "The main thing that both of them need to know is that I'm doing them a favor by hosting this reception. All they have to do is show up."

Melissa picked up her cheese Danish and took a bite. "That's a tough one. On one hand, you are doing a great thing by having this reception for them, but to take them out of the planning seems a bit harsh."

"I disagree. Think about it, most brides become bridezillas because they get overwhelmed with the planning and details. They're not able to enjoy the event most times because they're exhausted from all of the planning and details that have to be done."

"You make a good point," Melissa resigned.

"I know I do. Now, enough about Christian and his wife, what's going on with you?"

"The same ole thing, girl. Did I tell you I'm thinking about switching to a plant-based diet?"

"Yeah, right," Iris laughed. "Says the woman eating a cheese Danish and drinking coffee with cream."

"Don't laugh. I hear that switching is good for your body."

"I'm sure it is, but so is cutting out all of those sweets you love to indulge in. Getting off your butt helps too." Iris took another sip of her water.

"Girl, I'm not trying to be walking around here sickly. I'm already fabulous in my fifties, but I want to be sexy in my sixties and seventies. I plan on being around for a long time.

"I'm not knocking your decision. If that's what you want to do, by all means, go for it. I wish you the best. I'll stick to eating freshly caught fish in Maui." Iris shrugged and patted her hair on the ends.

Melissa sat up straight in her chair and folded her hands on the table. "I still can't believe Vincent surprised you with a trip to Hawaii. Girl, women dream of having a man to do that kind of stuff. I mean, I love Dean and all, but I wish he was able to do for me a fraction of the things Vincent does for you."

"I won't lie, that week in Hawaii was wonderful. It's not even about the money he spends. Vincent is good to me. He's kind and considerate and that man sure does know how to please. Whew." Iris sat and stared aimlessly.

"I know that look," Melissa teased.

"What look? What are you talking about?"

"Honey, you have stars in your eyes. Iris, you are in love with that man."

"What?" Iris attempted to sound shocked but she knew her friend was telling the truth.

"Don't even try to deny it. I've known you for a long time and I've seen you go through a lot of ups and downs. I know you are in love with that man." Melissa reached across the table and squeezed Iris' hand. "Does he know? I mean, have you told him?"

"I haven't told him. I'm scared to put myself out there and then find out he doesn't feel the same way. That would be devastating. But the signs are there. I'm sure he can look at me and tell. I love being around him. We don't have to go anywhere or do anything. I enjoy being in his presence. He's so easy to talk to and funny is not the word for him. The man is hilarious."

"Is it weird being with somebody that wealthy? I mean, it's not like you're broke. You live in Inglewood by choice. We both know that investing in Christian's company paid off big time for you, along with your other investments. I'm pretty sure you're not hurting for anything, but this man is a real deal billionaire."

Iris considered her friend's words. She was right, most people wouldn't know she was sitting on close to a million dollars. Yes, she dressed well, and drove a nice car, but she didn't flaunt her wealth. She lived what some of her friends considered a basic lifestyle. Her neighbors certainly had no idea of her financial standing.

"The real deal billionaire, as you call him, is a mere man. Yes, his outward appearance and lifestyle reflects his wealth, but to be in his presence away from the hustle and bustle of L.A., he's like anyone else. He doesn't allow his staff to wait on him hand and foot. If he's hungry, he'll go in the kitchen and fix himself something to eat. He makes his own bed, and when he's not working on a major project he does his own laundry."

"I'm telling you, he's a cool guy. Last week he took me to a special garage on his property where he keeps, of all things, a pickup truck. He said when he wants a break from the limelight, he'll drive that truck and go to a house he has in Fresno and spend some time. I love the fact that he doesn't treat me like I'm indebted to him because of the things he does for me. He's bought me a few things but nothing too extravagant. I believe we're building something real."

Melissa listened intently to her friend. Although Iris put up a rough exterior, Melissa knew how fragile she was. Seeing the way Christian's father had taken advantage of her and abused her, followed by the other men that came into her life only to use her for their benefit then leaving her heartbroken. She deserved to be happy. For years, Iris had given up on relationships altogether. Only going to dinner with a man occasionally, she'd stopped trying. Vincent came out of nowhere, her very own knight in shining armor.

"Iris, enjoy your relationship. Let down that wall that you're still holding up and tell him how you feel. You may be surprised to find out he feels the same way. You deserve it as much as anyone else. Let go of your inhibitions and receive the love that Vincent is giving. No matter what you

went through in the past, you need to know that you have a right to be happy and in love as much as anyone else."

Twenty One

"Mom, what is your flight number, and what time are you scheduled to arrive?" Shelby wedged her phone between her ear and her shoulder as she searched her purse for her headset with both hands.

"The flight number is 1018. Our itinerary says we should get there around 3:49 p.m. It's only me, Shanelle, and Shaunice coming on this flight."

"Why, where is Sheena?"

"Apparently this airline ain't good enough for her and her man. She claims they're flying first class on a different airline."

Shelby was livid. "Let me get this straight. I'm going to have to go back to the airport to pick them up, and she's bringing somebody that wasn't invited or accounted for?"

"Calm down, Shelby. No sense in getting yourself all upset over nothing. According to Sheena, they're supposed to be renting a car. And don't worry about the extra person. There's always somebody that doesn't show up for one reason or the other. Besides, the caterers always cook extra anyhow. It'll be okay."

"You're always defending her, Mama. Sheena is so freaking disrespectful. She gets on my nerves."

"Look, the reception is this weekend. Me and your sisters will be there tomorrow to help you with any final details. You'll see, everything will be fine so stop stressing."

Digging deep into the crevices of her purse, Shelby located her wireless headset. She placed it on her ear and slid the power button up, turning it on. "I don't know why I'm so stressed. It's not like I had to do a whole lot concerning the reception. I go for a final fitting of my gown tomorrow morning."

"You're going to be such a beautiful bride. You were beautiful on your wedding day, so I can only imagine what it will be like with all of that fancy planning Christian's mother and them rich folks are doing.

"Thank you, Mama. Yes, it will be fancy, and no doubt beautiful, but it won't be nearly as special as what you did for us. You used what you had, and you put your heart in it. Nothing compares to that."

"I enjoyed doing it for you. I love you, but now I need to get off this phone. I have so much stuff to get done before we leave here tomorrow and I still haven't packed yet. I'll call you tomorrow when we make it to the airport. Try to get some rest, and please stop stressing. You don't want to be looking like a hag on your big day. Everything is going to be okay."

Linda and Shelby ended their call. Glancing down at her watch, Shelby noted the time and went into the office. She made it a point to keep up with her school work despite the reception. Shelby sat down at the desk and rolled the chair closer. She noticed an email that Christian had printed out from a travel website. Her eyes clung to the page as she read the words seven days and six nights in Paris, France. She could barely contain her excitement. Was her husband

136

actually taking her to Paris, and why hadn't he mentioned it?

She jumped up from the desk and danced around the room. "Ooh la la, Qui, Qui, Madame." She raised her shoulders in an exaggerated motion as she spoke the common French phrases. "We're going to Paris," she said in a singsong tone. "Yes, yes, yes, I have the best husband in the world." Shelby jumped up in the air. She couldn't believe how much her life had changed.

~~☙~~

"Where is this girl?" Iris stood outside Francisco's boutique tapping her foot and checking her watch. Shelby's appointment for her final dress fitting was in five minutes and she didn't appear to be anywhere in sight. Iris turned to walk into the boutique when she heard someone call her name.

"I'm here, Ms. Tyler," Shelby yelled, further irritating her mother-in-law. "There was a traffic accident on the freeway and I couldn't get by. I got here as fast as I could."

Iris rolled her eyes, displaying her frustration. "You could have called, but that doesn't matter at this point. Let's get inside." She pulled on the door and walked inside with Shelby on her heels.

"Welcome, ladies," Francisco greeted. He clasped his hands together and turned to Shelby. "Are you ready for your final fitting, my dear?" He looked her up and down as if he was sizing her up.

"I sure am, Francisco. Lead the way." Shelby threw her head back and looped her arm through Francisco's waiting arm. He extended his other arm to Iris and they followed him to the fitting area.

The dress was a perfect fit. Shelby examined herself in the mirror and tears formed in the crevices of her eyes. "It's beautiful, Francisco. You did an amazing job." She turned to Iris who was staring up at her. "Do you like it, Ms. Tyler?" Shelby asked, almost pleading for her approval.

"Yes. You look stunning. My Christian is going to be so happy."

Shelby stepped off the small platform and ran over to Iris. She wrapped her arms around her and squeezed her tightly. "Thank you so much for all of this, Ms. Tyler."

Iris returned the hug. "You're welcome, Shelby." She broke free from Shelby's embrace. "Go ahead and get changed. I need to meet with Francisco at the front."

Francisco's assistant ushered Shelby back into the dressing room to help her change clothes.

Standing at the counter, Iris pulled out her credit card and handed it to Francisco. He accepted the card and placed it on the counter. "Would you like to see your dress, Ms. Tyler?"

"No, that won't be necessary," Iris replied. "As long as you made the alterations I suggested when I was here last week then it will be perfect."

"You know this is something that I don't typically do, but for you I'm making this exception. I hope it doesn't come back to bite me. I do have a reputation to uphold."

"Francisco, how long have I been doing business with you? You know I would never do anything to ruin your reputation. I want my son's reception to be unforgettable, and thanks to you it will be."

"I'm sure it will, honey." Francisco picked the credit card up from the counter and ran it through the scanner. He issued her a receipt and handed her the dress.

Moments later, Shelby joined them, carrying her dress. She noticed Iris holding a garment bag. "Ms. Tyler I didn't realize you were getting your dress from here, too. May I see it?"

"Maybe later. I'm late for an appointment right now and I must go. Your dress is already paid for so you can leave now as well. I'll call you later." Iris dashed out the door without so much as a backward glance.

Shelby stood with a puzzled expression. Francisco came from behind the counter and gave her a kiss on each side of her face. "I hope you will have a wonderful reception, Shelby. It was an honor having you as a client and when you have your next event, I hope you will consider me for your gown."

"Thank you, Francisco." Her phone rang before she could say anything else. She smiled at him and left the shop.

Shelby scurried to her car, hoping to make it before her phone stopped ringing. She tapped the screen to answer the call. "Hold on just a second, I'm getting in the car." Shelby dropped the phone into her purse and pressed the button to unlock her vehicle. Time was ticking and she needed everything to go right. She could hear the muffled sounds of the caller coming from her purse. Putting her dress on the hook in the back seat, she closed the door and slid in under the driver's seat.

She pulled her phone out of the purse and connected it to her car's hands free system. "Hey, Kim, what's going on?"

"Why are you so out of breath?" Kim asked.

"I was leaving the dress shop when you called. My hands were full so I was rushing to get in the car and to answer the phone. I didn't realize I was out of breath. Have you and

Julian made it to the airport?"

"That's why I'm calling you. The kids are sick. Julian doesn't want me to miss the reception so I'm coming without him."

"Are you serious?" Shelby tried not to show her irritation with Julian. She never quite understood why Kim chose to forgive and stay with him after his cheating fiasco, but who was she to judge. It was Kim's life and her marriage, therefore it was her choice.

"I know you're disappointed and I'm sorry. I was hoping he and I could enjoy this little getaway. God knows we could use it."

"What do you mean, y'all could use it. I thought you were going on weekly date nights and stuff."

"We do, Shelby, but it's a big difference between going on a date and taking a trip across the country."

"Why don't you get your mother-in-law to keep the kids so that Julian can come?" Shelby didn't want to be hard on her best friend but she didn't trust Julian. She was sure he had been working hard to find an excuse to keep him from coming to California. The only remorse Shelby had seen in Julian when he cheated on Kim was the fact that he had gotten caught. She was not convinced he had completely given up his extracurricular activities, better known as chasing women.

"I guess she could. I didn't bother to ask her because Julian said one of us needed to be home with the kids. I think it's some kind of stomach bug, because they can't keep anything down. Who knows."

"Whatever it is, please keep it there. I don't need you coming here getting me sick," Shelby said in a teasing tone, but she meant every word she spoke.

"Girl, I wouldn't do that to you. I do have some good news, though." Kim paused and allowed time for the anticipation to build. "Since Julian isn't coming, I asked Dominique if she wanted to come with me using his ticket since I booked a nonrefundable flight. I changed the departure time, since she couldn't get off work. Instead of arriving tonight, we will get there tomorrow afternoon. Now you can spend more alone time with your mom and sisters."

Shelby felt a little better. She would much rather spend time with Kim and Dominique than she would Julian. It had been a while since she got to hang out with her girls.

Iris and Vincent walked around the grounds. Vincent pointed out the area he had designated for the reception. "How are things going with the planning?" he asked.

"Things are going great. I have everything in place. We picked up our dresses today, and afterward I had a meeting with Kareena. Thank you so much for recommending her. She has been phenomenal. I told her what I wanted and she delivered."

"Did Shelby like her as well?"

"Oh, yeah, she did. I let Kareena know from the beginning that I liked things a certain way and she didn't take offense at all. She was able to get the linens in the color scheme and fabrics I wanted and the menu was exactly what I wanted." Iris bragged on Kareena nonstop concerning her willingness to meet Iris' desires.

"Sweetheart," Vincent said interrupting her. "You're going on and on about Kareena meeting your needs but what about the bride. Was she pleased as well? Did she have any input?"

"Of course she did," Iris chuckled, patting him on the arm. She and Christian had already had a cake tasting so she was able to tell Kareena what cake she wanted and what bakery

143

to use. This reception is going to be amazing. I've already finalized the guest list. There is so much work involved even though it's only a reception. I can honestly say, I'm glad they eloped because I would be worn completely out if I had to do a wedding and reception for them."

A raindrop fell and hit Vincent on the tip of his nose before he could respond. Additional drops fell causing them to run to the awaiting golf cart. The sudden shower pounded the top of the golf cart and soaked them and the grass. Vincent drove the cart to the main house and they ran in as quickly as they could.

Vincent grabbed a couple of towels and handed Iris one. "Where in the world did that rain come from?" Iris asked, while blotting her head, face, and arms dry.

"I don't know, but it was sudden for sure."

Iris pulled her moistened shirt away from her body. "Look at me, I'm soaked."

"I am too. This towel isn't getting it. Let's go upstairs and get out of these wet clothes."

"Ummhmmm, you just want to get me undressed." Iris smirked.

"That's not a bad idea," Vincent replied, smacking her on the butt.

They went upstairs to his bedroom and changed their clothes. Vincent pulled Iris into his arms and held her close. She laid her head on his chest, enjoying the feel of his hands rubbing her back.

"You're so good to me, Vincent. Where did you come from?"

"You mean originally or recently?"

"You're a mess. I don't know what I'm going to do with you."

"I can think of a few things, but for now I'd settle for a movie. Vincent took Iris by the hand and led her over to the sitting area of his bedroom. They sat down and he used the remote to turn the TV on.

Iris relaxed on the couch in Vincent's arms with her feet on an ottoman. She found so much pleasure in being with him. She was as content watching a movie on television as she was going to movie premieres. Iris thought back to her last conversation with Melissa. Perhaps it was time for her to reveal her true feelings.

The buzzing of her phone pulled her out of her musing. She grabbed her phone and swiped to answer. "Hello, this is Iris."

"Good afternoon, Ms. Tyler. This is Kareena, I hope I didn't catch you at a bad time."

"Hi, Kareena, what's going on?"

"I'm calling because I received a call from the rental company for the outdoor furniture. Apparently the forecast calls for rain for the next three days, which is going to cause the ground to be extremely soft and muddy. We need to change the reception to an indoor venue. I reached out to several venues and I'm pleased to say I have found an alternate location. It wasn't easy, given the short span of time, but I have secured it."

"Oh no, I was looking forward to having the reception on Mr. Garrett's property. Everything we have done was based on that. What is this new location that you have?"

Vincent tapped Iris on the arm gaining her attention. "What's going on?"

"Kareena, can you please hold the line for a brief moment?"

"Of course, Ms. Tyler."

Iris tapped the mute button on her phone and shared with Vincent the information that Kareena had just given her.

"It's not a problem, Iris. You can still have it here. We'll move everything inside. Tell her to proceed, using the house instead of the grounds. She's familiar with the layout."

Iris returned to her call with enthusiasm. "Kareena, don't worry about the alternate venue. Mr. Garrett has agreed to let us use the inside of the house due to the weather."

"Wonderful, I'll make the necessary changes. Thank you, Ms. Tyler. I'll see you in a few days."

She disconnected the call and placed her phone on a nearby table. Iris leaned down and kissed Vincent deeply. Pulling his shirt over his head, Iris straddled his lap. "Let me give you a proper thank you."

Twenty Three

"Girl, you outdid yourself this time," Melissa squealed as Iris gave her a tour of the reception space. The ceiling and walls were covered in sheer ivory and gold drapes. Crystal chandeliers sparkled throughout the room. The tables were covered in ivory tablecloths with dusty rose runners. Three foot tall crystal vases filled with roses, hydrangeas, oriental lilies, and orchids sat in the center of each table. The chairs were covered in dusty rose fabric.

"Thank you, Melissa. You know I had to do it up for my son."

"I love that gown you're wearing. Francisco is magnificent. Truth be told, all you need is a train on the back and you could be the bride."

"You're a mess, girl. You and Dean go ahead and find your seats. They're up front near the head table. I need to greet these other guests." Iris excused herself from her best friend and exited the room.

The car arrived carrying Shelby's mother and two of her sisters. She recognized them from the pictures Shelby had placed around the house. Iris rolled her eyes as they stepped out of the vehicle. When they got closer to where they could see her face, she plastered on a fake smile and extended her hand to Linda. "You must be Shelby's mother, she looks just like you. I'm Iris Tyler, Christian's mother."

147

Linda accepted her hand and shook it lightly. "That's a beautiful gown you're wearing, Iris. I've heard a lot about you. It's nice to be able to put a face to the name." Pushing her girls forward, she introduced them. "These are my daughters, Shanelle, and Shaunice. My other daughter, Sheena, should be here any moment."

"I see you like names that start with Sh," Iris stated with a giggle.

"I suppose I do," Linda replied, unamused. "Would you be so kind and direct me to my daughter?"

"I would, however, they haven't arrived yet. They aren't due for at least another twenty minutes. I wanted to give all of the guests time to arrive, mingle, and be seated before the happy couple makes their arrival."

"Oh, I see. In that case, I guess we'll go on inside."

"Mama, here comes Sheena," Shanelle said, tapping Linda on the shoulder.

"Who is that white man she's with?" Shaunice asked, louder than necessary.

Iris rolled her eyes in disgust. These people had no decorum in her opinion.

"I know she didn't bring that man up in here." Linda placed her hands on her hips and approached Sheena.

"How dare you bring this man to Shelby and Christian's reception, Sheena. Have you lost your mind?"

"Hello, Ms. Lamar. It's so nice to see you again," Thaddeus said, cutting into Linda's rant.

"Don't you, hello Ms. Lamar me. Sheena, you know good and well who this man is and what he's done to your sister. How dare you disgrace us like this?"

"Hello, to you too, Mama. Yes, I know who he is, he's my man. Plus, he didn't do nothing to Shelby, I wish y'all would

let that mess go. Shelby lied on him."

Iris watched the scene before her. She was so embarrassed. Her other guests were arriving and looked on in astonishment. She couldn't let this little fiasco, whatever it was, continue. She walked over to the group and cleared her throat, gaining their attention. "Excuse me everyone, we're about to get started. May I please get you all to come inside and take your seats."

"Gladly," Sheena said, looping her arm through Thaddeus' and walking into the mansion.

Vincent met Iris as she walked inside. He pulled her into his arms and kissed her. "You look stunning, my dear. I love that dress on you. The designer must have made it exclusively for you because no other woman could hold a candle to you in that gown."

Kareena approached and notified them of Christian and Shelby's arrival. They hurried to their seats and the staff closed the ballroom door. The band played romantic ballads that echoed throughout the room.

The doors opened and the DJ announced over the mic, "Everyone, put your hands together and welcome Mr. and Mrs. Christian Tyler."

A roaring applause went up from the crowd and oddly died out when Christian and Shelby entered the room. Guests looked from Shelby to Iris and back at Shelby. Shelby's mouth fell open when she spotted her mother-in-law. Stunned by what she saw, her feet felt like she was walking in wet cement.

"What's wrong?" Christian whispered in her ear.

"I can't believe your mother did this to me." Tears formed in her eyes but she refused to let them fall.

It wasn't until that moment that Christian realized his

wife and mother were wearing the same dress. Although Shelby's dress was a champagne color and his mother's gold, there was no mistaking the similarities of the gowns. "I can't believe her. Let's just get through this reception. I'll deal with her later." Christian gently tugged on Shelby's arm, ushering her to the front of the room.

Vincent looked at Shelby and then at Iris. He was stunned. He had never seen the groom's mother and the bride dress alike at any event, let alone a reception. He thought it strange but looking at the smile on Iris' face, he figured they planned it that way. He decided against saying something but made a mental note to ask her about it when they were alone later.

The orchestra played Johnny Gill's song 'My, My, My,' as Christian and Shelby shared their official first dance. Following the dance, dinner was served. Blake and Kim made speeches in honor of the couple. Linda gave a beautiful speech before Iris approached the microphone. She looked over at Christian who issued her a silent warning. She gave a short, yet sweet, speech and hurried back to her seat.

Christian and Shelby sat at the front of the room enjoying their meal. "This is a great turnout," Christian said to Shelby.

"Yeah, I don't know most of the people in this room, but they seem genuinely happy for us. Look at the gift table, it's overflowing."

"I'm amazed at how many people traveled here from Tenn…" Christian stopped in the middle of his sentence.

"What's wrong?" Shelby asked in a panic.

"What is he doing here?" Christian furrowed his eyebrows and squinted his eyes as he stared at Thaddeus Bierman, the man that had worked so hard to keep he and Shelby apart.

"I don't know why he's here." Shelby watched as her sister snuggled close to Thaddeus. "Don't tell me he's the rich boyfriend Sheena has been bragging to Mama about. I can't believe she brought that jerk here."

Christian started to rise from his seat, but Shelby placed her hand on his thigh to stop him. "No, don't, he's not worth it. Besides, if I can't act a fool with your mama about her wearing the same freaking gown that I'm wearing, then you don't get to act a fool over Thaddeus being here."

After dinner, the band cranked up the music and the party went into full swing. The dance floor was packed. The guests that weren't on the floor dancing, danced in their chairs, or laughed and talked among themselves.

Blake grabbed Dominique by the hand and pulled her close to him, dancing like they had known each other for years.

"Honey, you should maybe slow down on the drinking. You've taken in quite a bit," Shelby whispered into Christian's ear when he stumbled during their dance. He had gone through several glasses of champagne and a couple of shots with Blake.

"Loosen up, Shel. It's our reception. We're supposed to have a good time."

Shelby backed off. Between songs, Shelby leaned in to Christian, "I need to use the restroom, I'll be right back."

He nodded and turned his attention to Shelby's sisters, who were dancing alongside of him.

Thaddeus stood in the corner watching Shelby's every move. When Sheena pulled him onto the dance floor he danced with her, but continued to watch Shelby. He watched Shelby leave the room and figured it was the perfect opportunity for him to make his move. He waited a couple of moments before following behind her.

Winifred took note of the time and found Iris in the crowd. "Iris, this reception is great. You've done a wonderful job. I know Christian and Shelby are grateful. As much as I hate to leave, I need to get going."

"I understand. Give me a second and I'll walk you out." Iris placed her champagne glass on the table, and walked outside with her friend.

Shelby came out of the restroom and found Thaddeus waiting for her. "Excuse me," she said in an effort to get past him.

Thaddeus jumped in front of her, blocking her path. With every move she made, he interfered. "You look beautiful, Shelby. When are you going to end this sham of a marriage and come back home to Bethany with me?"

"What? Have you lost your mind? You clearly have been drinking too much. Get out of my way, Thaddeus, and go back in there with my sister. I knew you were only with her to get to me."

"Who, Sheena?" Thaddeus' words slurred. "That money hungry whore was an easy mark. You're the one I want, you know that. You always have been."

"Thaddeus, leave me alone." Shelby spoke through gritted teeth.

Iris walked back into the mansion and noticed Shelby and Thaddeus. She stood still, making sure her shoes wouldn't make a sound on the floor, revealing her presence. She couldn't hear what they were saying, but based on their body language, they were both deeply involved in the conversation.

"I love you, Shelby. I'm the one you were supposed to marry. You and I both know it. I'm never going to let you go." Thaddeus grabbed her by both arms and kissed her on the lips.

Iris gasped and ran into the ballroom to get Christian. Without regard to the guests, she yelled, "Christian, I told you that good for nothing trollop was after your money. She's out there kissing her sister's boyfriend right now. I knew she didn't love you."

"What?" Christian pushed Iris aside and ran toward the ballroom's exit.

"Get off me, Thaddeus," Shelby roared. Freeing herself from his grip, she slapped him across his face and rushed toward the ballroom. She was met by Christian, Iris, and Sheena.

"What's going on out here?" Christian yelled.

"Baby," Shelby called out, reaching for Christian.

Christian slapped her hand away, "Don't baby me. My mom told me you were out here kissing this clown."

"Shelby, you out here pushing up on my man?" Sheena interjected.

"Sheena, shut up. You should have never brought him here to begin with," Shelby barked.

"Man, it's not what you think," Thaddeus said, struggling to string his words together.

"Oh, it's not, huh?" A loud pop echoed though the hall as Christian's fist made contact with Thaddeus' face. "You must think I'm stupid."

"Christian!" Shelby screamed.

"I can't believe you, Shelby. How could you?" Christian pushed the mansion door open while the guests stood around watching the drama unfold.

Shelby ran out behind him. "Christian, I didn't do anything. He kissed me, but…"

"I'm done, Shelby. I guess my mom was right after all."

Christian pulled his keys out of his pocket and jogged to his car. He pulled out from the curb, leaving black tire tracks on the brick driveway.

Shelby dropped to her knees in front of the mansion and sobbed. Her mother came to her side and kneeled down, wrapping her arms around her. "I didn't do anything. I love Christian. I would never betray him."

Vincent grabbed Iris by the shoulder and turned her to face him. "You did this. All of it. How could you be so cruel? This is too much. I can't deal with it." He turned and walked away. He stopped by the door where his staff was standing and instructed Simon to ask the guests to leave. Vincent walked upstairs to the west wing. He entered his bedroom and closed the door.

Christian pressed the gas pedal as hard as he could. The further he could get away from Shelby and Thaddeus the better. How could he be so stupid. He ignored all the signs blinded by his own love for his wife. Tears burned his eyes, further impairing his already inebriated vision. The blare of car horns, followed by a loud crash, was the last sound he heard.

Shelby parked the car at the curb, and stepped around to open the passenger side door. The orderly pushed the wheelchair up to the car and helped Christian climb inside. Shelby strapped him in and closed the door. With his right arm and his left leg in a cast, it was almost impossible for him to do anything without assistance.

The ride home was painful and nerve wrecking. After spending a week in the hospital, Christian was cranky and nervous. Every time Shelby approached an intersection where the light was turning red, he flinched. If she ran over a pothole or he felt like she was taking too long to put on breaks behind another vehicle, he yelled at her.

"Christian, I know this is hard for you, but I need you to try to calm down. We're almost home. I promise I will take good care of you." Shelby leaned over and kissed Christian on the cheek. Her cell phone rang and Iris' name displayed on the screen. She looked over at Christian. "Do you want me to answer it?"

"No, I told you I don't want to talk to her. I wish she would stop calling."

"Christian, she's your mother. I know she's concerned about you."

"If she was so concerned, she wouldn't have started this mess. The way she handled things was wrong. If she thought you were cheating on me, she didn't have to blurt it out in front of everyone, causing a scene. My mother took advantage of the fact that I had been drinking. She knew when she approached me the way that she did that I would be upset and react. She did that on purpose. She wanted to humiliate you, and because of it, I'm sitting here with a shattered thigh and broken arm."

Shelby knew it was best to end the conversation. For the past week, she had heard it over and over again. Christian was not interested in forgiving his mother. Shelby couldn't blame him for his ill feelings toward Iris. Their reception turned out to be a complete nightmare. After Christian left, she was forced to deal with all the judgmental stares of the people.

Iris had continued to berate her, calling her a gold-digging slut, which almost brought her and Shelby's mom to blows. Sheena foolishly rushed to Thaddeus' aide, driving a further wedge between Shelby and her family. The scene was pure chaos.

Shelby was left to ride home with her mother and sisters, only to get a call saying Christian had been involved in a horrible car accident. The hospital had also called Iris since both she and Shelby were listed in his phone as emergency contacts.

When they arrived at the hospital, Christian initially refused to see any of them. He was taken into emergency surgery due to the multiple fractures and internal bleeding. When he came out of recovery, he asked the nurse to bring his wife in and to send his mother away. Shelby, still wearing the gown from the reception, held his hand and wept. She explained to him what really happened between her and Thaddeus and her reaction to the kiss that Iris failed to see.

Shelby pulled up at their house and pulled the car into the garage. Knowing he would be coming home in a wheelchair, she had a small ramp installed to assist Christian with getting in and out of the house. She pulled the wheelchair from the trunk and helped him get into it. Her heart broke, seeing her husband so vulnerable and in such pain.

She got him into the house and pushed his chair into the downstairs master bedroom. The bed was full of pillows. She helped him change clothes and get into bed. Thankfully, the pain medication was starting to kick in and made him drowsy. Shelby placed a pillow underneath his leg and kissed him. "I'm going to fix us something to eat. Try to get some rest."

Christian nodded and closed his eyes. Shelby slipped out of the room and located her cell phone. She pulled up her contacts and tapped the screen to make the call. "Hi, Ms. Tyler, this is Shelby."

"I called the hospital and they told me Christian had been discharged. Where is my son?"

"He's here resting. We were in the car when you called but he didn't want me to answer. He's still pretty upset. Maybe now that he's home and away from the poking and prodding of the nurses he will relax and finally take your calls."

"This is ridiculous. I can't believe you've managed to turn my son against me. You'll get yours, Shelby. That's not a threat but a promise."

"Wait a minute, Ms. Tyler. I have remained silent despite all the things you have done to try to hurt me. I would never try to turn Christian against you. This is your doing. All of it. Remember, I was the one keeping you updated on his condition when he was in the hospital. Your dislike for me

157

has caused you to create the rift between you and Christian. I love my husband and he knows it. You just refuse to accept the fact that he could be happy with someone other than you. It's time you stop blaming me and acknowledge your own actions. Hold yourself accountable for a change. Goodbye!" Shelby disconnected the call before Iris could say another word.

Iris threw her phone across the room and dropped to her knees. She was devastated. How could Shelby talk to her that way? Who did she think she was? Tears began to pour out of her eyes like water from a faucet. How had her life changed so dramatically? In such a short time, she had lost her son and her man and it was all because of Shelby.

She had attempted to contact Vincent on several occasions but he wouldn't answer nor would he return her calls. It was like he fell off the face of the earth. The last words he had spoken to her were, 'This is too much.' He turned away and never looked back. She was ushered out of the house, along with the rest of the guests. Hadn't their relationship meant anything to him?

If she was in her presence she would kill Shelby with her bare hands. She had singlehandedly taken everything away from her that Iris loved. The doorbell rang, commanding her attention. "Go away," Iris yelled. The ringing continued with more urgency. "I said, go away."

The sound of a key in the lock frightened her. She knew it couldn't be her son because he was in no shape to come to her house. Iris' heart pounded. Could it be Shelby coming to finish her off for good? She jumped up from the floor and ran to her bedroom. With shaky hands, she entered the combination to remove her gun from the locked box in her nightstand drawer.

"What are you doing?" the close proximity of the voice scared Iris, drawing a bloodcurdling scream from her lungs. "Stop being so dramatic. That's what your butt gets for not answering the door. I bet you forgot about the spare key you gave me for emergencies."

Iris turned and saw her best friend in the doorway. "Girl, you scared me half to death. Have you lost your mind? I could have shot you."

"I'm sure you could have if you can ever get the box opened. The way you're over there fumbling, if I was someone trying to do harm to you, you would have been got."

Melissa joined her friend in the room and sat on the side of her bed. "I've been trying to call you, and since you didn't answer I came over here to make sure you hadn't done anything crazy. What are you in here doing anyway?"

Iris joined Melissa on the bed. "Everything is so messed up. That woman has taken everything from me. Most importantly, my son. I just don't understand." Iris brought her hands to her face and bawled openly.

Rising from the bed, Melissa retrieved a box of tissues from Iris' dresser and handed it to her. She hated to see her friend so broken, but she owed it to her to be honest. "Iris, you have to stop this, honey. I love you and because I love you, I have to tell you the truth. Shelby didn't do this. She didn't do any of it. I tried to warn you when you started this mess. The reception was your chance to bring unity to your family. You chose to flip it into exactly what it was."

Melissa got up and paced the floor. Iris' eyes bore into her. "I don't doubt that you'll want to dismiss me after this, but I have to say it anyway. You chose to exclude Shelby from the planning of the reception, then you had Francisco to create a duplicate dress for you knowing everyone would see your dress before they saw Shelby's. That was low. But then with the way you ran into the ballroom yelling and telling Christian Shelby was kissing another man, that was overkill."

"I guess you're blaming me for the accident too, huh? I know what I saw, Melissa. I didn't make that up. She was kissing that man."

"You saw what you wanted to see. I'll bet you didn't know Shelby had filed a sexual harassment claim against that man when she was in Tennessee. You didn't pay attention to the fact that her mother and sisters refused to allow him and her other sister to sit with them. You were too busy being upset that her girlfriends from Tennessee were changing seats with them."

"How do you know all of this, Melissa?"

"Because, unlike you, I spent time with them. I talked to them both at the reception and at the hospital. They are good people. You just refuse to give them a chance."

"I lost my son and my man because of her. I won't forgive her for that. I don't care what you say."

"You haven't lost Christian. He's just upset with you right now. He'll come around. You may have lost your man, but it's not because of her, it's because of you. That man is a billionaire. He can have any woman he wants. He chose you and you screwed it up with your antics. He owns a major television studio, so I'm sure he sees enough drama on the movies he produces. He doesn't need to see it in his own home. He probably feels like he can't trust you."

Iris jumped up from the bed. "You can say what you want, but I refuse to believe it. I was good to Vincent and I've always cared for my son."

"Look, I'm only telling you this because I love you and I want you to be happy. Hopefully, you can turn this thing around before it's too late. In order for that to happen you have to accept your part in it. Apologize and make it right. Christian could have died in that accident. It's clear he isn't going to leave his wife."

"If this is all you came for, you can leave. You're my best friend and I love you, but I don't have time for this right now."

Melissa disregarded Iris' statement. "Do you want to go and get something to eat? You need to get out of this house. It's driving you crazy."

"Did you hear what I said? No, I don't want to go and get something to eat. I want you to leave. I'm fine right here."

"Fine. You're only putting me out because you know I'm right. That's okay, I still love you. When you're ready to act like the fifty something year old woman that you are, give me a call." Melissa turned and walked away without another word. She didn't even bother to look back at her friend. Some things it would take God himself to fix.

Twenty Five

"Sweetheart, you're doing so good." Shelby gushed, watching Christian slowly walk from the bedroom to the home office.

His recovery was hard, but he had worked diligently with his physical therapist to minimize his recovery time. Christian turned on his computer and scrolled through unread emails. He called Shantrice and gave her instructions on how to respond to the messages.

The doorbell rang and Shelby made her way to the door. She had been expecting her guest for quite a while. She held her breath as she opened the door. The woman walked in and wrapped her arms around Shelby tightly, catching her off guard.

"Thank you so much for allowing me to come by. Is there somewhere we can go and talk…alone?"

"Sure." Shelby stepped back and allowed Iris to enter the house. "Christian is in the office, so we can go outside by the pool.

Iris gave Shelby a nod and followed her outside.

Shelby reached into the fridge on the way out and grabbed two bottles of water. She handed one to Iris and twisted the top on the other one. They took a seat in the lounge area and Shelby turned her bottle up for a deep gulp. "How have you been, Ms. Tyler?"

"I've been okay. I can't believe it's been a month since we've seen each other. How's my son?"

"He's doing better. He no longer needs the wheelchair, which is a huge improvement. He hated that thing and I hated seeing him in it. We still have to sleep downstairs, but he says it's not a big deal since that's where he slept before we got married."

"Oh, I see." Iris opened her water bottle and took a sip. "Look, Shelby, I don't want to beat around the bush. I came here today to apologize to you. I was wrong for everything that I did to you and Christian. I shouldn't have interfered. I've lost a whole month with you two because of my selfishness. I didn't believe someone could meet and fall in love so quickly without there being an ulterior motive. It was easy for me to judge you, because I didn't know you."

"Ms. Tyler…"

Iris held up her hand, "Please, let me finish. My son means everything to me. He's all I ever had that I knew was mine. Then you came along and our family of two changed without my input. That was difficult for me. I didn't know how to move forward with you in the picture. So, I made some poor choices."

"Over this past month I've done a lot of thinking. I realized, despite everything that happened, you've never disrespected me. You were great at the clothing drive. You treated everyone there with dignity and respect. You and I both know the fashion show was as successful as it was because of you." Iris placed her bottle on the table and looked into Shelby's eyes. "I visited your school looking for you and found out you had taken a leave of absence to care for Christian. A selfish woman wouldn't have done that. I'm glad my son has you. And if you'll have me, I'll be honored to be your mother-in-law. Please forgive me, Shelby."

"Of course, I forgive you, Ms. Tyler." Shelby stood up from her chair and took a seat next to Iris. She hugged her, and soon felt the moisture from Iris' tears on her shoulder.

"Shelby, where are you?" Christian's voice echoed. He leaned on the kitchen counter for support before taking a seat on the stool.

Shelby ran inside to aid her husband. "I'm here, honey/ I was outside talking…"

While Shelby spoke, Iris stepped inside and approached her and Christian. "Hello, son. How are you?"

"Mom, hi."

Iris rushed over to him and put her arms around him.

"What are you doing here?" His words were laced in bitterness.

"She came to apologize," Shelby interjected. "That's why we were outside. Your mother was apologizing to me."

Christian looked at his mother in disbelief. "Is that true, Mom? You came over here to apologize to Shelby?"

"And to you. Son, I was wrong, dead wrong, and I can't tell you how sorry I am. I'll do all I can to make it up to the both of you. I miss you and I want to be back in your life. Please forgive me."

Christian took his good arm and wrapped it around his mother. "Of course, I forgive you. I've missed you too."

Shelby put her hands together. It felt good seeing her husband and his mother reunited. Although he tried to keep it from her, Shelby knew the estrangement between Christian and her mother-in-law was wearing on him.

The three left the kitchen and gathered in the living room. They spent the remainder of the day together talking and enjoying each other's company. Iris loved being with her son and daughter-in-law. She would never admit it to anyone, but inwardly she wanted what they had.

"I'm glad you decided to start back going on our weekly walks. I missed being out here inhaling the fresh air." Melissa spread her arms wide toward the sky and took a deep breath.

"Girl, stop being so dramatic," Iris teased, causing them both to laugh. "It does feel good being out here." They came to the waterfall and took a seat on a nearby bench.

They watched as other hikers maneuvered the terrain. Some walked in pairs or small groups while others chose to take the walk alone. "This has been a crazy year. Time is passing by so quickly. How is Christian doing?"

"He's good. Shelby took him last week to have the casts removed. He said he was going back to work in the office this week. He's been working from home, but I know he was driving himself and her crazy being there."

"I'll bet he was. When Dean is sick he drives me nuts. Girl, he is the biggest baby, acting like he can barely move. He only gets out of bed to use the restroom, and a shower is out of the question."

Iris turned up her lip. "I don't envy you with that."

Melissa stood and extended her hand to pull Iris up. "I won't lie, he picks that last nerve and works it, but I wouldn't take anything for him. What can I say, I love him." Melissa hunched her shoulders as they walked in the direction of their vehicles. "Have you heard from Vincent?"

"No." Iris' expression turned somber. "It was fun while it lasted. I know one thing, if the next man can't make me feel the way Vincent did when we were together, he doesn't stand a chance."

"I know that's right," Melissa agreed, giving Iris a high five.

The ladies arrived at their vehicles and did a light stretch. "This was our laziest walk ever." Iris looked at her fitness tracker. "I only got 3,200 steps. That's a thousand steps less than I normally get. I'm not going to complain. I wouldn't mind a nice cup of coffee. How about we go to the coffee shop. It's not like we sweated today."

"That sounds good to me. I could go for a candy apple latte." Melissa pulled on her shirt, "Are we going like this, in our workout clothes?"

"Why not, it's just coffee."

"Oh, I know you've changed because you've never gone to that coffee shop in athletic clothes. You'd be too afraid of somebody we know seeing you."

"Well, today is a new day and I want coffee, so let's go."

"Okay, girl," Melissa replied, snapping her fingers twice.

Ina watched as Iris and Melissa entered the coffee shop and took a seat at their usual table. She lightly shook her head. How could their timing be so perfect? Her last patrons had just vacated the table. She shuffled over to them with her tablet in hand. "Hello, ladies. Long time no see."

"Hi, Ina, how are you doing today?" Iris replied.

"I'm well. Are you two on your way to the gym?" Ina asked, pointing at their outfits.

"No, we're not," Iris snapped.

"We went walking in the park," Melissa said with a smile

combating the bite in Iris' tone.

"Oh, I see. What would you like to order today?"

They gave Ina their order and chatted while they waited for her to return. Iris was focusing on a text message and didn't notice the people that entered the coffee shop. Melissa kicked her foot under the table, causing her to look up.

"Ouch," she exclaimed, ready to let Melissa have it when their eyes met.

Vincent stopped and turned in their direction.

"Hello, Vincent," Melissa said, extending her hand to him.

"How are you?" he replied, shaking her hand, but focusing on Iris. "Hello, Iris."

"Hi, Vincent." Her heartbeat was so strong it echoed in her ears. She didn't know how she would feel when she saw him again. With his sudden appearance, she no longer had to guess. Her heart ached, longing for his touch and the bond they once shared. Iris pushed back her chair and stood. "Vincent, can we talk for a moment?"

Vincent hesitated before answering. "Sure. Why not."

Iris stepped in front of him and walked out the door. Vincent followed. They made it outside and walked to her car. "How have you been?" she asked, hoping to ease the tension.

"I've been okay, and you?"

"I don't really know how to answer that. On one hand, I could say I've been good. I was able to apologize to Christian and Shelby. Thank God my relationship with them has been restored. But, there is a big chunk of me still missing."

"Why is that?"

"Because I never got the chance to apologize to you. I feel horrible about everything that happened with the reception.

I realize I completely embarrassed myself and most of all I embarrassed you. You were kind by allowing me to host the reception at your home. But, my need for control caused me to ruin the best relationship I've ever experienced. I miss you so much."

"Iris, I, I don't know what to say. That was a lot to deal with. I've worked hard in my career and in building my reputation. Some of my business associates were there. I don't really know how to recover from that."

Her eyes filled with tears before one escaped. She quickly swiped the tear away. "I understand, and I don't expect you to change how you feel. I consider it a blessing to have seen you today, because I could finally tell you I'm sorry. Thank you for the time we shared. I'll forever cherish it. I love you, Vincent, and our being apart won't change that. Thank you for showing me what could've been."

Vincent dropped his head. He opened his mouth, but no words came out. When he found his voice he said, "It's okay. We live and we learn. I'm glad things are better between you and your family. I really do wish you the best." He reached down and embraced Iris before walking away.

Melissa looked through the window and noticed Vincent walking back into the coffee shop without Iris. She grabbed their handbags and left enough money on the table to cover their drinks. She rushed outside and found her friend sitting inside her car crying. "Iris, what happened?"

"It's over, Melissa, it's really over. I tried to make it right, I tried to apologize but he walked away. I've lost him for good."

Twenty Seven

"Mr. Garrett, your car is ready, sir."

"Thank you, Simon." Vincent grabbed his bag and headed out the door. He climbed into the back of the Town car and instructed the driver to take him to the airport. He needed to get away, to clear his head.

They arrived at the airport and the driver pulled up to his jet. He parked the car and got out to open the door for Vincent. The pilot, along with the co-pilot and flight attendant, greeted him and confirmed his travel plans.

Vincent settled in his seat and pulled out his iPad. He scanned emails and read through documents he had downloaded. Surrendering to the comfort of the plane, he reclined in his seat and slept.

The sound of the tires hitting the pavement awoke him. He sat up and looked around. He checked his watch, making sure they hadn't made an unscheduled stop.

"Welcome to Maui, Mr. Garrett," the flight attendant said. She handed him his bag and waited for him to exit the plane.

Another driver waited outside the plane to take him to the inn. Following the Twenty minute drive, they arrived at The Inn at Mama's. Vincent walked into the lobby and approached the counter. "My name is Vincent Garrett and I would like to check in please."

The clerk greeted him, and replied, "Yes, Mr. Garrett we have you down for our one bedroom beachfront suite."

"No that's not correct. I requested the one bedroom cottage."

The clerk frowned. "Let me see what happened, I apologize." He tapped on the computer, searching the reservation records. "It appears you were upgraded, sir. You are among our VIP guest."

"I appreciate the kind gesture; however, I would prefer the cottage."

"I'm sorry, Mr. Garrett. We have no other vacancies. The suite is all that we have available."

"Fine, I've had a long flight, and I would like to get settled in." Vincent took the access card from the clerk and had the driver to take him to the room. He closed the door and dropped his head. The last time he was in this room, Iris was with him. He tried to shake away the memory but it was so vivid that he could almost see her walking throughout the space. Every inch of the room reminded him of her.

Vincent tossed his bag on the bed and went into the bathroom to take a shower. The warm water pounded his body from every angle. He closed his eyes and reminisced on the shower he and Iris took together. The sound of her laughter filled his ears.

"This is too much, get it together," he said aloud, rubbing his hand across his head. He finished his shower and got dressed. He couldn't wait to get out of the room. Vincent laughed thinking himself to be ridiculous.

Hunger pangs created audible sounds as he walked along the beach and headed over to Mama's Fish House to grab a

bite to eat. He was starting to feel like Maui was a bad choice for him to unwind. He sat at the bar and ordered a drink. Two scantily clad women approached him.

"Hey, handsome. Are you here alone?"

"As a matter of fact, I am," Vincent answered, thinking the women were the distraction he needed.

"Not anymore," one of the women said in a seductive tone, garnering giggles from her companion. They took a seat on either side of him and greedily devoured the drinks Vincent ordered for them.

He entertained their company until his eyes grew tired. "I'm going to my room now ladies, I've enjoyed your company."

"Why does the party have to end? We don't have a curfew. Let's take the party to your room."

Vincent considered their offer. He had been drinking, but he was not drunk. He knew what they expected to happen if they went to his room. He also knew from past experiences that they could not be trusted. "You ladies are gorgeous, but unfortunately, I'll have to pass. I'm tired and I won't be any good to you tonight." Vincent paid the check, and left the disappointed women sitting at the bar where they found him.

He returned to the room and laid across the bed. His mind drifted to Iris and lingered. He couldn't deny his love for her. She was full of drama, but he had never experienced the joy that he had with her with any other woman in his life. Not even his late wife whom he loved dearly. Vincent felt like he couldn't live without Iris, but somehow, he'd managed to walk away from her, not once, but twice. He knew he'd hurt her.

Vincent thought he had gotten over Iris, until he saw

her at the coffee shop. When she told him she loved him, he wanted to break, but his pride wouldn't allow it. He sat up in the middle of the bed and shook his head. What was more important? His pride or his chance for happiness? Iris had asked him to forgive her, but in truth he was the one in need of forgiveness. He loved her and he didn't want to spend another day without her.

The sun began to rise over the ocean. Vincent called his driver and his pilot. He told them he needed to return to Los Angeles right away. Within an hour he was in the air. The six-hour flight felt like an eternity. He tried to relax, but he couldn't. He rehearsed what he would say to her over and over in his mind.

The plane landed and Vincent had his driver to take him straight to Iris' house. He had only been there a few times to pick her up. He gave the driver the address and tapped his foot in anticipation of his arrival. They pulled into Iris' driveway and Vincent jumped out of the car. He rang the doorbell and started banging on the door at the same time.

"Who is it?" Iris called from inside.

Vincent continued to ring the bell and bang.

Iris approached the door with caution and looked out of the side window. "Vincent," she whispered in disbelief. She pulled open the door and Vincent rushed inside, taking her into his arms. He hugged her close and then stepped back, holding her hand.

"Iris, baby, you're not in this alone. When we last saw each other, you told me you loved me. You asked for my forgiveness, but I should have been asking for yours. I was so caught up in maintaining my image that I failed to see past the moment. I've never loved any woman as much as I love you, and I don't want to spend another day without

you. Marry me, Iris. Be my wife. I love you, Iris. Say yes, please say yes."

Iris stared at Vincent in disbelief. Was this happening? Was he really there?

"Don't leave me hanging, please say something."

"Yes, Vincent. I'll marry you." Tears fell from her eyes, "I love you so much. I'll marry you."

He pulled her into his arms and kissed her with a passion she had never experienced.

~~⌘~~

"May I have this dance?"

"Of course, you may." Iris placed her hand in Christian's hand and followed him out to the dance floor."

Christian held his mother as they swayed back and forth to the beat of the music. "You are the most beautiful bride in all of California, Mom."

"Thank you, son. You're so sweet. I thought this day would never come for me. I'm here today because of you. If you hadn't been willing to fight for your love for Shelby, I wouldn't have believed that true love was possible. I tried for years to make it work with your daddy."

"I know you did, Mom. You don't have to explain."

"Please let me finish. Your father was my first real relationship. He was the only man that I had ever loved. He was so mean to me, and he took advantage of both me and you. Through the years I've dated other men, but I never expected much. I know I made a lot of mistakes when it came to you and Shelby. I'm so grateful that the two of you forgave me."

"When I met Vincent, I wouldn't allow myself to feel the

love that I had for him because I kept telling myself nothing would come of it. I didn't think I was good enough for him. Losing him and you made me realize just how blessed I was when you all were in my life, including Shelby. When I made things right, I still felt a void because I didn't have Vincent. Son, I can't put into words the joy I felt when he showed up at my house telling me how much he loved me. When he asked me to marry him, I gladly accepted because by then I realized I was worthy of love."

"May we cut in?" Vincent asked as he twirled Shelby out of his arms and pulled Iris by the hand. "Sweetheart, we have to go, our plane is waiting."

Christian turned Shelby's back toward him and wrapped his arms around her waist. "Mom, before you go, we have a gift for you. Shelby held out a small box to Iris.

Iris opened the box and her eyes widened as she studied the contents.

"You're going to be a grandmother," Christian said, kissing Shelby on the cheek.

"I'm going to be a what!" Iris yelled as Vincent caught her before she hit the floor.

The End

Note From The Author

Thank you for reading Worthy of Love. This story is the sequel to my novel Journey to Love. I thoroughly enjoyed writing this story. I hope you enjoyed it as well. Although Iris' antics were hilarious, she hurt those that loved her. The moral of this story is, if you focus all your attention on someone else's life you may miss out on what God has for you. God has blessings in store for each of us. Don't miss your blessing by interfering with another's.

If you enjoyed this novel and would like to help support the series, the best thing you can do is leave a review at Amazon, Goodreads, or even your personal blog — reviews help other readers determine if a book is to their liking. Authors, rely on such word of mouth to get our books in front of new readers.

You can also join my email mailing list at http://bit.ly/LAmailing. The list receives no more than one or two emails per month, with updates on my next book, as well as recommendations of other authors you might like.

In the words of the old song, If I can help somebody as I travel along, then my living shall not be in vain.

Blessings,
LaCricia

About the Author

LaCricia A'ngelle is a licensed Evangelist, Author, and Publisher. A native of Chicago, she currently resides in Georgia with her husband and children.

To arrange signings, book events, speaking engagements, or to send comments to the author please email her at: author@lacriciaangelle.com

Connect with LaCricia A'ngelle online at:
www.lacriciaangelle.com
www.facebook.com/lacriciaangelle or
www.facebook.com/authorlacricia
Twitter: @authorlacricia
Instagram: @lacricia_angelle

Check out my other books!

Girl, Naw!
It Ain't Over

<u>First Lady Series</u>
Positive Deception
Lina's Redemption (coming Spring 2018)

Journey to Love

Sophomore Mom

The Christmas Gift (short story)

www.ingramcontent.com/pod-product-compliance
Lightning Source LLC
Chambersburg PA
CBHW030336180626
46810CB00003B/1384